1795

D1294185

FOR THE SAKE OF HIS PEOPLE

John Wijngaards, 1935 -

McCrimmons

Great Wakering Essex

First published in Great Britain by McCrimmons, Great Wakering, Essex in 1990.

Copyright (c) John Wijngaards 1990.

ISBN 0 85597 467 2

Printed and bound by Billings & Sons.
Artwork for cover by Linda Schwab.
Art lettering by Leigh Hurlock.

'The use of violence is incompatible with the Tao; and whoever opposes the Tao will die young.'

LAO TZU

ONE

'Yuddhapalli looks so tranquil today', Jim said to Sundari. 'A model village. A haven of peace.'

Sundari just shook her head.

She was right. A haven of peace, indeed! As if its deadly conflicts did not exist. A windstill ocean - carrying a cyclone in its womb. An idyllic mountain - nurturing an explosive volcano. Jim wondered if Yuddhapalli was different in this respect from the other six hundred thousand villages that cover the Indian subcontinent . . . .

From their vantage point on the flat roof of Sundari's two-story high girls' secondary school, they surveyed the familiar rural scenes. Coolies filling jute bags with a day's crop from a cotton field. Children dawdling home from school, playing on the way. Women balancing on their heads jars of water filled at a nearby well. A toddy tapper clambering up a tall palm tree and beginning to collect the juice from a funnel-shaped pot inserted in the tree's crown. Two oxen lazily pulling a cart heaped high with fodder.

Suddenly a ripple of activity ran through the village. A woman came out of a house. She seemed unsure of herself, dishevelled and disoriented. She looked furtively around in all directions, then walked down one of the main streets into the centre of the village. Two men appeared as if from nowhere and followed her from a distance. It was as if they had been waiting for her. They made no sound but their threat was tangible.

'Trouble', Sundari whispered.

Jim ran down the two flights of stairs that took him to ground level.

'Wait!' Sundari called after him, but he was already outside walking in the direction he had seen the woman go. He saw neither her nor the two men that shadowed her. But he knew they could not be far off, for the street was electric with tension. People stood in their houses, staring through the gateways to their compounds or from behind small, stone windows. They had sensed the menace. They were a silent crowd, anticipating the shock and the thrill of an act of violence.

Jim found her a little further on, huddled on the steps of the small shrine to Pothamma, the pre-Arian mother goddess. The iron gate to the shrine was closed. The woman sat holding the gate with both hands, leaning on its trellis and looking at the idol inside with a wordless prayer.

Hearing Jim's steps, she turned round. In spite of her face being drawn and distorted by fright, its features were strikingly beautiful. She looked at Jim, ran down the steps and fell at his feet, clasping his knees to beg for protection. Jim did not know what to do. He bent low to raise her up but before he could do so, the woman shrank back in terror. The men were there, four of them now, silent and threatening.

Jim braced himself for a fight. They were strong and easily his match. He looked round for a way out. He saw that the gate, though carrying a padlock and key was not actually locked. He jumped towards it, pushed the gate open, took the woman by the hand and dragged her inside.

It had been his plan to close the gate but he was too late. The men had come inside too. While two pinned him down to the ground, the other two approached the woman who had hurled herself at the feet of the short bronze idol. The men dragged her away, answering her pleas and protests with grim silence.

Jim struggled to get loose but failed. As soon as they had their prisoner outside, the two men who were holding Jim let go, jumped up and closed the gate behind them. One slid the bolt into place, fitted the padlock, turned the key and took it out. Jim was a prisoner, furious to see the woman being dragged away to an uncertain fate.

He shouted and cried. Only a deep silence was the re-

6

sponse. He tried to scale the gate or the fence but they were high and spiked. Five minutes passed before Sundari turned up, another ten minutes before she had retrieved the key and could let him out.

'What's it all about?' he asked Sundari.

'Adultery', she said. 'The woman was caught red-handed, perhaps led into a trap.'

'What will they do to her?'

Sundari looked away.

Jim insisted they go to the woman's house. He hoped there was still something he could do for her.

When they got near, they heard loud weeping. They went inside the house. The woman lay on a mat in the middle of the half-lit room, surrounded by female relatives. Her eyes were closed. Her face was blotched and blue. Her hair and sari were soaking wet. Her body was limp, she was dead.

'They say she committed suicide, jumped into a well.'

'Did she?'

'Who can prove otherwise?'

Jim pushed his way into the middle, knelt down next to the body and closed his eyes. He had failed. The woman had turned to him and he had not been able to save her.

She had not known he was a priest. But she had instinctively recognised he would be different. She had appealed to him as one human being to another, as so many people had appealed to Christ. But he had miserably failed her. She was dead.

With an agonising clarity he remembered a previous occasion on which he had failed. On that day too he had knelt beside a body - in that drab upstairs flat of 58 Mariner Street in Londonderry . . . .

It had all begun on a dull winter afternoon in 1974. Jim O'Brien had been a young priest at the time, assistant in St. Mary Magdalene parish, Bishop Street, Londonderry.

The housekeeper had called him from the shed at the back of the rectory where he was repairing his bicycle.

'There's a woman in the parlour, Father. Seems in a bad way.'

'Thanks, Joyce. Tell her I won't be a minute.'

Joyce's warning had not really prepared him for the sight of emaciation and human misery the visitor offered. Tall she was and stately. But so thin and pale. Wide blue eyes in hollow sockets framed by a white, freckled face. Everything about her was clean, but shoddy: her straggling red hair, her torn mauve shirt over dark blue slacks, her gym shoes with tattered edges. She looked anxiously at Jim, her left hand resting on a ramshackle pram.

'What's your name?' Jim said, offering his hand.

'Rosaleen. Rosaleen Donovan.'

'Sit down.'

She slumped back in the chair and closed her eyes. She radiated an infinity of tiredness. As if she had not slept for days. She must be twenty-five, Jim guessed. Attractive in spite of her run down condition. With a pronounced sense of guilt Jim contrasted his own health and fitness with her obvious frailty.

'Do you belong to our parish?'

'Yes, Father.'

'Where d'ye live?'

'Mariner Street.'

'I've never seen you at Mass.' He regretted his words almost as soon as he uttered them.

'How could I go, being ill and all and having three kids at home? I'm just up from having had Kate.'

'What can I do for you?'

'I'm worried about my husband. Kevin.'

'What about him?'

'He's gone. Three days ago. Didn't say a word to me. I'm worried.'

'Did you have a row? Has he walked out on you?'

'We're always having rows, like. When he comes home

pissed. But he wouldn't go like that. It's not like him.'

'What does he do for a job?'

'He's an electrician. Unemployed most of the time. We're on the dole the whole year round.'

'Did you tell the police?'

'How can I? They wouldn't lift a finger to help .... And I don't want them to put their nose in. It may be that the boys are behind it.'

'The boys' was the going term for the Provos, members of the Provisional IRA.

'Oh? Is he working for them?'

'He hasn't much choice, has he?'

'What does he do?'

'Dunno. He never tells me.'

He could read fear, if not despair, on her face. Instinctively he felt she was not telling him everything, could not tell him everything. He knew the signs only too well. Pity got hold of him. He made up his mind to help. She turned to him in her hour of need.

'What d'ye want me to do?'

'Find him. For Godssake.'

'Wait', he had said. He himself had gone to the kitchen and made her a cup of coffee and two sandwiches. When he returned with the tray, he found Rosaleen had uncovered one breast and was feeding her baby.

She looked at him to see if he would mind.

He smiled.

Diocesan instructions were unequivocal. Priests should stay clear from the IRA and from other militant nationalist groups. But Jim had strong ties with the movement. An uncle of his had fought the Black and Tans. His father, in Belfast, was a member of the Irish Liberation Front, a splinter group with a deadly effective organisation.

9

Jim did not even consider confiding in Father O'Flaherty, his parish priest. For all his nationalist sympathies O'Flaherty would never agree to his assistant flouting the Bishop's explicit instructions. Nor would Jim enlist the help of his father. That would only reinforce the feelings of dependence and inferiority he had resented throughout his adolescence. He had to strike out on his own. With the details Rosaleen had furnished he should be able to make a start.

He arranged to see Hugh McCormack, a travelling salesman, in the Fayrie Queen. Hugh was reputed to have links with the IRA and, though he rarely went to church, had helped the parish on a number of occasions. Mainly to please his wife Helen Jim suspected. She was a regular churchgoer and relished nothing as much as going to Lourdes on pilgrimage.

Over a glass of guinness Jim explained his concern.

Hugh eyes him speculatively.

'You're asking for inside information. In some quarters that would be frowned upon, not half.'

'I only want to help Rosaleen.'

'If the boys come to know, Rosaleen too would be in trouble. They might discipline her for indiscretion.'

'It's that hot, hey?'

'Could be.'

'Where do I go from here?'

'Difficult to say. It may have nothing to do with the volunteers. Perhaps the Brits have picked him up. Or the police, on some minor offence.'

'Christ!'

'You could make some discreet enquiries, of course.'

'With whom?'

'With Gerry Kelly, landlord of Columba's Cross. He's our area man. Bound to be in the know one way or the other. But be careful.'

'Why?'

'He's a tricky man, Gerry is. Extremely sensitive. Has a cruel streak in him. Keep Rosaleen out at all costs. He could be vindictive.'

10

At dinner that evening Jim asked his parish priest about Gerry Kelly. If anything could be known about anybody in his parish, Father O'Flaherty knew.

'God help us! That scoundrel? What have you let yourself in for?'

'Is he that bad?'

'Vicious. Mean. A bully. Owns a lot of houses near the pub. Exploits his tenants. He's got some standing with the boys and uses it to terrorise people. Stay away from him.'

'What about his wife?'

'What's the interest?'

'The Sisters in Mount Carmel school are planning to organise a fete and a jumble sale', Jim improvised, using information that had just come to his notice. 'We wondered if some of our Bogside pubs could sponsor a darts' competition.'

'Well, Gerry Kelly will be no use, I tell you. Nor will Nora, his wife. They're Scrooges, the pair of them. Stay clear. That's what I say.'

Jim knew he could not stay clear.

TWO

That same evening Jim dropped in at Columba's Cross for a drink. The pub was well attended. He said Hello to a few people he knew then moved straight to the bar. The landlord came over.

'A guinness, please.'

The man was well-built, in his fifties, shifty eyes in a flabby face.

'Are you Gerry Kelly?'

'Who else? And you're the new assistant in St. Mary's.'

'Right.'

'I haven't seen you here before.'

'Nor have I seen you in church.'

'Nor will you, Father', Gerry laughed. 'Until my funeral, who knows.'

'Forget it! We're not in the business of burying bloody pagans.'

Gerry laughed again.

'I've come to talk business, not to convert you.'

'What about?'

'Can't we talk, somewhere private like?'

'Right!'

Gerry gave a sign to Nora his wife, then gestured for Jim to come round the bar.

'Go through here.'

He ushered Jim into a small room behind the bar.

'You can speak.'

'You know Kevin Donovan of 58 Mariner Street? It's just round the corner.'

'What about him?'

'D'ye know him?'

'Of course, I know him. I know everybody in my patch. What's up?'

'He's disappeared. Gone. Three days ago. Was working on a job in the priests' house. Left things half done and scarpered. I went round to his wife. Doesn't have a clue.'

'Why come to me?'

'Let's stop playing games. I know what I know and you know now that I know. Where's Kev?'

Gerry narrowed his eyes.

'You're bloody cheeky talking to me like that.'

'Don't be daft. I'm not interfering like. If you tell me you know, I'll stop worrying.'

Gerry shifted in his seat.

'As it is, I don't. It's odd. Him going like that without letting me know. But I can find out. I'll put a word around.'

'If you don't know, I'm worried', Jim said again. 'Let me know the result of your enquiries.'

'I may or I may not', Gerry replied.

'When can I come again?'

'Drop in tomorrow by ten.'

Next morning, before going to see Gerry, Jim decided to visit Rosaleen. 58 Mariner Street turned out to be a small house converted into three flats. The Donovans lived at the top.

When Jim rang the bell, the door was opened by Finbar O'Neill, an old-age pensioner Jim had seen in church and who occupied the ground floor. Finbar told him to go up two flights of stairs.

Jim knocked on the apartment door.

There was scuffling inside. A crying child being beaten. Then Rosaleen's voice.

13

'Who's there?'

'Me. Jim O'Brien. The priest.'

'Go away.'

'I have to see you.'

'Did you find Kevin?'

'You want me to talk on the stairs?'

'Wait. Let me get decent.'

Five minutes later Rosaleen opened the door. Her face was bruised on one side. A cut ran across her cheek. One eye was hardly visible behind an ugly red swelling.

'My God!' Jim said. 'Who's done that to you?'

'Come in.'

Jim entered the living room. Children's clothes, toys, household articles were scattered everywhere : on the window sills, the threadbare sofa, the table, the chairs, everywhere on the mat. Two toddlers - Bernie and Melanie Jim learned later - were playing in a corner, subdued, fear in their eyes.

'I'm sorry about the mess', Rosaleen said. 'I can't cope.'

She was near breaking point.

'Who's been belting you?' Jim said as soon as they sat down.

She did not reply.

'Not Kevin?'

She shook her head. 'Kevin can get rough when he's pissed. He won't hit me.'

'Who has?'

No answer.

'How can I help you if you don't tell me?'

There was genuine sympathy in Jim's voice. He looked around. He must give her a hand. Deeds would speak more than words.

'You think about my question', he told her.

He went round the house, putting things in order. He collected the dirty plates and cups and carried them to the kitchen sink. The toys went into one corner. He picked up bits and pieces of clothing, unwashed nappies, handkerchiefs, underwear and piled them in a heap. He brought out the vacuum

14

cleaner and hoovered the room. He moved into the kitchen, did an emergency washing up, sponged down the sink and the table as well as he could.

Rosaleen sat in her chair, crying, holding her head.

'I'm so ashamed, Father', she said once or twice. But she did not get up. She was utterly exhausted. All she did was to hold her hand on Bernie and Melanie, occasionally patting them or stroking their hair.

'I'm only doing what Kevin should have done and he's not here', Jim stated. 'Moreover, I'll talk to Eileen Prendergast, our social worker. She'll come around and help you for a couple of days.'

'Thank you, Father.'

'Now tell me: who's given you a hiding? Has it to do with Kevin?'

Rosaleen sighed.

'You'll keep it to yourself?'

'Sure.'

'Gerry Kelly came last night.'

'Gerry Kelly?'

'Gerry Kelly. You know him?'

Jim's blood began to boil. The bastard!

'Tell me!'

'Don't tell him I told you. He'll kill me.'

'I won't. Tell me what he did.'

'Gerry Kelly is Kevin's link man for the boys. He'd come to know Kevin has gone. He scolded me for not letting him know immediately.'

'And then?'

'He kind of grabbed me, shoved his hand up my leg and wanted sex. I kicked at him. He hit me. You see, he's our landlord and he's tried before when he comes down to collect the rent. But I've never let him. This time he beat me real bad, threw me on the bed and raped me.'

'The pig!' Jim said.

'I feel so dirty, so unclean .... Why do us women always have to feel dirty? Either we've got periods or we're forced to have sex . . . . I'm sorry two of my kids are girls.'

It was the old, Jansenistic view of sex so prevalent among Catholics, Jim knew. Full of concern he sat down next to her and held her by the hand.

'Listen to me. You don't need to feel dirty. You can be proud to be a woman and a mother. Our Blessed Lady herself had periods. She too was a mother. And being raped is no sin. You couldn't help it. Many saints have been raped and have gone high to heaven.'

Rosaleen stared at him to take it in.

'The nuns at school or your mum may have told you a woman's sex is Eve's curse, or rot like that. They were wrong, I'm telling you. I'm a priest. You don't need to be ashamed of yourself. We'll talk about this some other time. And about the rape, forget it. You don't even need to confess it for it was no sin on your part.'

That's my after-rape counselling, Jim thought. *Totally inadequate.* But what else could he say? He knew that he would not easily get her to discuss this kind of thing with a social worker.

Abruptly he got up.

'I have to go now. You better look after your kids. I hear Kate is yelling in the bedroom. I'll ask Eileen to give you a hand.'

On the way down Jim stopped to talk to Finbar.

'Kevin's been missing since four days.'

'I've noticed, Father.'

'Where could he be?'

'I've no idea. Kelly came here last night asking the same question.'

Jim looked at Finbar.

'Rosaleen's in a bad way. We've got to help her.'

'Yes, Father.'

Jim had already passed out of the front door when Finbar

16

called after him.

'Yes?'

'Perhaps Molly might know more about it. She lives on the first floor.'

'What makes you think so?'

'Some comings and goings on the day Kevin left.'

'Is Molly in?'

'No.'

'Where can I meet her?'

'She works in a supermarket in Rossville Street. Sainsbury's.'

'What's her full name?'

'Molly Fennell.'

'Thanks.'

Suppressing his inner fury, Jim walked into the pub and confronted Gerry. They were alone.

Shifty-eyed as usual, Gerry started the conversation.

'Hi, Father! Bad news!'

'What bad news?'

'About Kevin. I've decided to tell you as it's not one of our own operations. Someone of Kevin's description was picked up by the MR some days ago. They're holding him for interrogation.'

'Who the hell are the MR?'

'A branch of the Secret Service. UDR. Very special, very much underground. We don't know why they went for Kevin. Frankly, I don't like it.'

'What are you going to do about it?'

He shrugged his shoulders.

'Even if we were to do something, would you expect me to tell you?'

'No', Jim said.

'A final warning. Stay away from Rosaleen, Kevin's wife. It

would add complications.'

The pig! Blood rose to Jim's face in anger. But remembering his promise to Rosaleen he turned on his heel and walked out.

What next?

THREE

In the light of Gerry's parting word on Rosaleen, it seemed imperative to provide her with immediate protection. Imagine Gerry going there again .... !

Jim tracked down Eileen Prendergast, told her as much as was necessary to enlist her cooperation and received the assurance Rosaleen would be looked after.

Back in the priests' house, Flaherty bawled at Jim because he was late for two infant baptisms that had been booked.

Jim went across to the church, pacified the two irate families, conducted a joint baptismal service for them, signed the register and left other formalities to the sacristan. He left word with the housekeeper that he had received a call from the hospital ....

Free once more, Jim took his bicycle and rode to Rossville Street. He felt a great sense of urgency. Life was cheap in Ulster and between the various conflicting forces someone like Kevin could be an easy victim. He could be tortured by security men, then conveniently disposed of. He might be killed by the IRA if they were afraid he might grass on them. Never before had he felt that people's wellbeing: Kevin's, Rosaleen's, their children, depended so much on himself.

Enquiries about Molly Fennell in Sainsbury's revealed that she worked in the butcher's carvery. He gained admittance and found her slicing ham and wrapping it in plastic packages.

Self confident and good looking, with auburn hair jumping around her face, she radiated vitality and impudence. She looked Jim over with frank interest, apparently liked what she saw and announced she would take her lunch break now. Five minutes later they sat with a sandwich and a cup of tea in a deserted corner of the canteen.

'Oh my, you're not used to girls like me', she said, enjoying Jim's discomfort as he could not help observing her generous breasts under her see-through blouse. 'Come on, what can I do?'

Jim explained his concern about Kevin and Rosaleen.

Molly bit her lip, serious for one moment.

'Why come to me?'

'There were goings on in your place the day Kevin left.'

'I'll tell you', Molly said after a while. 'I'll tell you because Rosaleen's a poor bitch, a real skivvy. Kevin's hard on her. He wants sex all the time. He doesn't let her take pills or a shield because he says sex's no fun if you can't get a girl banged up.'

'My mum too is weighed down with me dad and fourteen kids', Molly continued. 'She's just a breeding machine. Always sick with having a baby or losing one. And the priest stuck up for me dad who's only interest was laying her all the time.'

She glared at Jim. 'I dunno if you're like that. You're all the same, I s'pose, frigid y'self and envious of other people's sex.'

Jim became red in the face, but he did not reply.

'It does you mighty good to hear the truth, anyway, even from a slut like me.'

She looked to see if the word made an impression.

'Yes, I'm a slut, you see, a whore. Prigs like you turn up their nose at me but I don't feel that way. When I ran away from home, I had no option but to start walking the streets. 'Playing the field', they called it. I had feelings of guilt at first. But when I found out what goes on in real life, I dropped my guilt and decided to use sex.

'All men are the same: the provos, the hoods, the police, the Brits. They all want sex. I want to get married some time. To a feller I like. When I've saved the money for it, not to depend on him.

'In the beginning I went round like a real bitch, running after the men. I needed cash. I made sure not to get bothered with a wain. I got one all the same, mind you, Oliver, three years ago. I've left him with one of my sisters to look after, for cash of course.

'Then I got this job so I could be more selective. And this is where Kevin comes in. Since last Christmas I've been working evenings as a stripper, over the river in Waterside. It's good fun, really. You're on this stage with all the lights on you, dancing to a tune and pulling off one piece of dress after the other, teasing like. The men love it and I feel great the way they look at my body. When I drop my knickers, the lights go off and I scamper. Ten pounds for fifteen minutes' work.

'Some days ago a man was waiting for me outside. They do that at times if they take a fancy to you. I let myself be picked up if they look decent and can pay. This time it was a Brit, young, tall, handsome. He wanted to take pictures of me, he said. In the nude. He would give me a hundred pounds.

'Why not? I said. Having to pose in the nude and all, I took him home. I got his cash. He took out his camera and made me undress. Then suddenly he got out a whip and threatened me. I knew then he was kinky. I screamed. Kevin was just coming up the stairs. He opened the door, saw me standing starkers and this fellow with the whip in front of me.

'They fought, the two of them. Kevin gave him a hiding and threw him out. He may not have told Rosaleen for she always thinks he's after me. Which he is. The next day he'd gone.'

'Who was the Brit?' Jim asked.

'I wish I knew who the fucker was', she said. 'He was tall and lean. Called himself Ian. A soldier I'm sure. That kind of age. English accent. I wouldn't be surprised if he didn't belong to the Enfield barracks in Waterside. A lot of them go to the striptease place I work in.'

'Any other clues?'

'He's got a moustache. Prim and proper like . . . . Hang on! He left a brolly. Forgot to pick it up in the scuffle of getting out. It's at the back of my door.'

'Good', Jim said. 'Let's look at it. Time is short.'

'I can't leave now. I've got to go back to work.'

'But I can't wait till this evening . . . . '

'Alright', she said. 'You won't rob me. Here's my keys. Give them to Finbar after picking up the brolly.'

'Thanks', Jim said. 'When all the fuss is over I'll see you some time. Not for sex but to get a few points straight. For now, you've been great.'

As fast as he could Jim cycled back to Mariner Street. With Molly's keys he let himself into the house, then into her apartment. He found the umbrella hanging behind the door, as Molly had said. He spread it open. He was in luck. It carried a small tag with the initials I.R.

Suppose Molly's hunch was right? Suppose Ian came from the Enfield barracks?

Leaving Molly's keys with Finbar, he jumped on his bike again, crossed the river Foyle by Craigavon bridge and reached the barracks twenty minutes later.

It took some argument and being frisked before he was admitted to the quartermaster.

'One of your men left an umbrella, initials I.R. His name is Ian. He's tall and has a moustache.'

'That can only be Ian Reynolds, the sergeant. Give it to me, I'll return it to him.'

'I want to speak to Reynolds.'

The quartermaster raised his eyebrows.

'All right.'

A few minutes later Jim was ushered into a parlour where Sergeant Reynolds, smartly dressed in full uniform was standing at the window, waiting for him. He was tall and handsome, with a tiny moustache. It had to be the man.

'Does this umbrella belong to you?'

The sergeant looked at it, then shook his head.

Jim decided to be brutal.

'Last Tuesday you picked up a prostitute after a striptease show. You offered to pay a hundred pounds for being allowed to take pictures of her in the nude. Her name is Molly Fennell.

You went to her flat in Mariner Street. You began to use a whip on her but a neighbour threw you out. That neighbour, Kevin Donovan, has now disappeared. What have you done to him?'

Sergeant Reynolds did not blink an eyelid.

'You're talking tommy rot. I'm a happily married man. I never picked up a prostitute. I've never been in Mariner Street. Get out!'

'I have witnesses.'

'I have witnesses to testify that I was on duty the whole of Tuesday evening.'

Jim almost exploded with anger.

'I want to see your commanding officer.'

'Very well. This way, please.'

Walking behind the unruffled sergeant Jim began to feel he was losing ground.

He was let into the office of Major Campbell-Hart, who rose to shake hands and offered him a seat. The sergeant withdrew. Jim explained the matter once more.

'Thank you for telling me, Father', the major said when Jim had concluded. 'The whole story sounds highly improbable. Sergeant Reynolds is a devoted family man and has an impeccable record. I will check though.'

He left the office and returned in ten minutes' time.

'You have no case at all. Reynolds was on duty the whole of Tuesday evening until midnight.'

'But I've got witnesses and the umbrella!'

The major dismissed this evidence out of hand. When Jim threatened to leak information about the incident to the press, the major in turn threatened with libel.

'Look here', Jim said. 'I'm not trying to nail your man for his devious sex. I'm concerned about Kevin Donovan. He's disappeared. I want to know where he is.'

'As likely as not it's your own people who've put him out of the way. I'm afraid I have to ask you to go. That's all the time I can give you.'

Jim got up, his Celtic temper making him boil.

'My father always says you're worse than hoods who mug old-age pensioners and rob lonely women. He's right. You're bloody hypocrites. You talk of equality but all you do is back up the Loyalists and suppress Catholics. You talk of justice but don't care a damn about what happens to my people - so long as you protect that dirty, lecherous sergeant of yours. One day the people of this country will rise to a man and take justice into their own hands .... '

'Enough', the major said, his face grim with anger.

He rang the bell. Jim was escorted outside.

He realised with bitterness he was no nearer to Kevin.

FOUR

Jim was convinced Ian was behind Kevin's disappearance. The information Gerry had given him pointed in the same direction. Ian was taking revenge through some friends in the MR . . . .

The IRA would not help him. Might pose a threat to Kevin, in fact. The only people who could possibly help were the ILF, the Irish Liberation Front, to which his father belonged. He would have to swallow his pride. Give his father a ring. Preferably from a phone booth, for extra security.

He found a pay phone near Craigavon Bridge and dialled the Belfast container terminal where his father was employed. The response was instantaneous.

'Container Cargo Limited.'

'I want to speak to Noel O'Brien.'

'We don't take calls for employees.'

'This is urgent. I'm Father Jim O'Brien, his son, calling from Derry.'

There was a grunt. Then, 'O.K. Hang on . . . . '

Three minutes later his father was on the phone, bawling as usual.

'What the bloody hell do you ring me here for?'

'For Godssake, stop shouting. I need your help.'

'So? What for?'

'Can't explain it fully . . . . Can people there hear my voice?'

'No. Carry on.'

'A friend of mine has been kidnapped by a loyalist gang. I can't go to the police. Where can I go?'

There was a silence on the other side. Then his father spoke again.

'Don't go anywhere. Stay put. The mountain will come to Mohammed . . . . And don't bloody phone me again at this number!'

The phone was slammed down on the other side. Jim realised that the final outburst had been for the benefit of the receptionist. If the mountain was coming to Mohammed, someone of the ILF would approach him . . . . He decided his first duty was to return to Rosaleen.

He found Rosaleen's apartment in much better shape. Eileen Prendergast had done a good job. Rosaleen too seemed more relaxed.

'Can ye wait a wee while?' she asked Jim. 'I'm in the middle of giving the kids a bath.'

'Don't mind me', Jim said. 'I'm used to family baths. You just carry on. We can talk while the kids soak.'

'Right', she said, with the first smile Jim had seen on her face. 'But don't blame me if you get soaked yerself.'

The warning was in earnest. Bernie and Melanie, standing in half a foot of soapy water, splashed them as soon as they entered. Rosaleen was wearing an apron. Jim got a generous dose on his trousers. The children shrieked with joy. Playing in the bath was family fun time.

Jim rose to the occasion, dismissing any immediate thought of serious discussion. He played along, splashing back and dodging Bernie's and Melanie's concerted attacks as well as he could. The damage had been done anyway. Black clergyman's trousers do not take kindly to soap marks. Finally he helped to rub Bernie dry while Rosaleen worked on Melanie.

'Any news of Kevin?' Rosaleen asked when both children, glowing with satisfaction, had been put on high chairs in anticipation of the evening meal.

'Yes and no.'

'Tell me.'

'I can't tell you everything - for your own sake. Some group, a loyalist outfit, may be holding Kevin. It has nothing to do with the IRA. At least, so I believe. It may be some act of personal grudge. On the night before he disappeared Kevin rescued a woman who was being molested by a man.'

'He never told me anything about it', Rosaleen said ruefully.

'He didn't want to upset you.'

Rosaleen did not reply. All the joy had gone from her face, and her posture.

'What have they done to him?'

'I don't know. They haven't killed him, for sure. If they had wanted to kill him, they would have shot him and left his body.'

Rosaleen fell silent again and began to weep. The children too caught her mood. First Bernie started to cry, and then Melanie. Both stretched out their hands to Rosaleen. She took both children from their high chairs and kept them on her lap to dry their tears.

'Who's bothered about people like us?' she said to Jim in between sobs. 'Who's bothered? We're always on our own, me and my kids. Kevin's away. He doesn't tell me what he's up to most of the time. I can't ask the peelers because Kevin is involved. I can't ask the provos - they'll get us into more trouble.'

'I'm trying to help', Jim said softly.

'I know. But you're the Church.'

'So what?'

'The Church always lets us down. In the end.'

'No . . . . surely not!'

'Always. In the real trouble that is. From IRA trouble or police trouble the priests wash their hands.'

'Come on!' Jim said. 'You know that isn't true.'

'It is. Kev always says, with real trouble you're on your own. When Jesus Christ was being crucified his priests ran away. They left him to die on his own. That's what they do to the likes of us, he says.'

Jim fell silent. He thought of the instruction of the Bishops forbidding priests to have any involvement with the IRA or related groups. Perhaps she was right. People were often left alone in their darkest hour. That was how his father felt about it . . . .

At supper that evening Father Flaherty harangued Jim on the need for an assistant priest to be available, accessible, around, on call.

'This morning you were late for the baptisms. This afternoon you were not here to take a sick call. Mrs. Edwards in St. Mary's Hospital. Just as well I didn't wait for you to turn up. I'd hardly finished giving her the last sacraments before she passed away. What would have happened if I'd not been here?'

Jim looked contrite. Flaherty was right. It had been his day on duty. He had not been expecting any emergencies. He told Flaherty so.

'Wrong, my son! Wrong! You should always expect emergencies. You know Murphy's law: if things can go wrong, they will; at the most awkward time. Let me now teach you Flaherty's law: people die when you least expect them to. They'll live a thousand years when you're fully prepared, then take the great plunge as soon as you've turned your back.'

'I'll remember, Father', Jim said.

A little later he managed to steer the conversation in his direction.

'How far should a priest go to help people?'

'Like what?'

'Like if the police is after them and they're carrying guns? Could we shelter them?'

'Hide them? My God! Become accessories to whatever they've done? You must be out of your mind. I hope you're talking of a hypothetical case . . . . '

28

'Of course.'

'Then why do you raise the point?'

'Well, I was reading about South America, liberation theology and so on. In Chile, for instance, the police terrorise the people. In the slums there are small resistance groups. Some of these people who were armed with guns were pursued by the police. They took refuge with the parish priest, a missionary from Germany. He gave them shelter and hid their weapons because he knew they wouldn't get a fair deal from the police.'

'Risky business', Flaherty commented.

'Sure, risky. But should a priest not take risks for his people?'

'It all depends what kind of risk.'

'Don't you think it could happen here?'

Flaherty looked at Jim with suspicion in his eyes.

'You're not preparing me for some goddamn stupid thing you've let yourself in for?'

'No, no Father!' Jim said laughing.

'Well, you never know with these young guys coming out of the seminary nowadays. But let me tell you one thing: if ever I find a gun, a hand grenade, or even a pen knife or anything else that could be lethal in this house I'll be on the phone next minute and hand you over to the police.'

'You'd never do a thing like that!' Jim protested.

'I might not', Flaherty conceded. 'But I sure would get rid of the stuff pronto, and you as well!'

Next morning after eight o'clock Mass Rosaleen was in the sacristy, waiting for Jim.

'Kevin came back last night.'

'That's marvellous!'

'He's changed. He doesn't speak a word. I can see he's been beaten all over. He's scared of something real bad.

Please, come and talk to him. He's in some deep trouble and can't get out.'

'I'll come', Jim promised.

'Don't tell him I asked you to come. I told him I'd go out to do some shopping.'

'I won't', Jim said. 'What's more, I'll go there now. Give me half an hour to talk to him before coming back. He may want to talk to me alone.'

Kevin did not seem in a mood to talk to anyone when Jim knocked on the apartment door shortly afterwards. Half dressed and unshaven, he almost shoved Jim out of the door as soon as he saw he was a priest.

'So you're Kevin', Jim said, pushing his way in. 'Nice lad you are, leaving your wife like that. She was worried sick.'

'It's none of your business.'

'Of course it's my business. It may not have penetrated your skull but there are people who care. Well, what can I do for you?'

'What d'ye mean?'

'Come off it! I know where you've been. The MR kidnapped you. What did they want?'

'Jesus Christ!' Kevin said. 'How do you know?'

He sat down on the sofa, exhausted, his face in despair.

'If *you* know . . . . Who told you?'

'Gerry Kelly', Jim said taking a seat opposite him.

'My God!'

'I've been trying to find out where you were. Gerry told me you'd been picked up by the MR. From Molly I heard about your scuffle with the Brit. Did he take revenge?'

'Who? Oh, that bastard. No . . . . '

'Then, what happened.'

'Father, leave me. Get out of here. It was mighty good of you to try to help. But you've got me into a load of trouble by talking to Gerry . . . . '

'Why don't you tell me what it's all about', Jim said. 'I want to get you and Rosaleen out of this mess. Besides, if I got you into trouble by talking to Gerry, I want to repair the damage. I know Gerry is a nasty piece of work.'

Kevin looked at Jim.

'I mean what I say', Jim continued. 'You can spill the beans. You've heard about the seal of confession and all that .... I may be the only neutral party you'll ever meet. And if I can, I'll help you.'

Jim could see that his words did not fail to make an impression on Kevin. The man was in desperate need of an ally, someone to confide in.

'I'll tell you, Father', he said. 'I have been condemned to death.'

FIVE

'Start from the beginning', Jim said.

'I've done some jobs for the provos, small jobs like wiring up bombs, checking electrical connections. I'd like to stay out really but then someone has to do the job I suppose and Gerry leans heavy on me. He's our landlord. We depend on him, especially as we're out of cash most of the time. But I've never been on an outside job, if you know what I mean. I've never planted a bomb. They wouldn't trust me to.

'The MR somehow has got the idea I'm the great explosives expert. They took me in to make a deal. They've heard that the provos have some new kind of plastic explosive from Eastern Europe. I don't know the first thing about it, but I let on I did. To get away from them. They want a sample of the stuff.'

'And you promised to get them some?'

'I had to. I'd no choice I tell you. They'd have rubbed me out if they thought I couldn't deliver. Now I'm lost. I can't deliver. If I don't, they'll kill either me or Rosaleen, they said.'

'Can't you tell Gerry? Surely the provos will help you out.'

'They won't. They'll think I've squealed. If they know the MR held me and let me go, they'll guess I've made a deal. And Gerry is a bastard. He's got an eye on Rosaleen and he'll be happy to find any excuse to get rid of me.'

Jim thought for a while.

'Look here, I may be able to help you with the provos. You remember what happened in Molly's room? The fellow you flung out of her apartment?'

'I do.'

'Tell them you were held and beaten up in personal revenge. Molly will back you up. I have his name and address. It will let you off the hook as far as they're concerned.'

'Perhaps', Kevin said.

'Meanwhile we can think about the other crowd . . . . What precisely did you promise?'

'They told me to deliver two pounds of the stuff in three days' time to an address in Locksmith Gardens.'

'And you've nothing to give them?'

'Exactly. And Gerry won't trust me. He'll have me tailed wherever I go. If they think I'm a tout, I'm finished.'

'I may come up with something', Jim said. 'Stay calm. Keep Gerry happy for the moment. This evening or tomorrow morning I'll drop in again, with some positive plan I hope.'

All that day, while going about his routine business, Jim thought about Kevin's and Rosaleen's plight. There did not seem to be a way out. As Kevin said, unless a miracle happened, he was condemned to death.

In the afternoon an elderly gentleman came to see him.

'I'm Bill', he said. 'A friend of your father's.'

'Oh', Jim said.

'I heard you're in a spot of trouble. Perhaps I can be of help to you.'

Jim hesitated.

'Is it something affecting you personally?'

'No', Jim said.

'What is it? I can't prescribe the medicine, if I don't know the disease.'

'Quite so', Jim said. 'But matters have become more complicated. I've had to promise secrecy. I wish I could explain the whole thing but I can't.'

'Then I won't be of much use to you.'

'Could you come back tomorrow?' Jim asked. 'I have to clear some matters first.'

'I'm afraid not.'

'I could get in touch with you.'

'No. We trust your father but we have no experience of you. It's our business to trust nobody we don't know. This is your chance. Tell your story or you're on your own.'

'Very well', Jim said. 'I can't tell you. That's it. Thank you for coming.'

'You've got your dad's temper', the gentleman said, smiling.

Jim was sorry when he saw him go.

Was it the last chance of outside help?

That night Jim could not sleep. The hours were ticking by and he was no nearer a solution.

At one o'clock he got out of bed, put on trousers and a pullover and walked downstairs. He opened the kitchen door and made himself a drink. His frustration angered him. He needed to do something!

Prayer - of course!

He finished his drink and walked through the passage way that led from the priests' house into the church. He unlocked the door and entered the dark church. He went to switch on the lights, but then stopped himself. He waited till his eyes were accustomed to the dark. Then he walked to the middle aisle and faced the altar.

The flame of the sanctuary lamp threw moving shadows on the walls. It was eerie. Powerfully mysterious and beautiful.

He fell on his knees.

'God', he said, 'Show me what I have to do. You haven't made me a priest for nothing. I want to help these people. I'm at a loss.'

He prayed in silence.

Inspiration did not come.

From sheer restlessness and also because he was getting cold, he began to walk up and down the aisle, reviewing as he had done so often that day, the various angles of the situation.

Rosaleen's words came back to him.

'The Church always lets us down. In the end.'

'With real trouble you're on your own.'
*'When Jesus Christ was being crucified, his priests ran away.
They left him to die on his own.'*

Jim halted before the altar, right underneath the giant crucifix suspended above it. In the dancing shadows of the sanctuary lamp, Christ's body on the cross looked even more twisted
and grotesque than usual.

Running away was the last thing he wanted to do.

As a priest he wanted to be loyal to his people, even die for
them as Christ had done. 'No man has greater love than he
who gives his life for his friends', Jesus had said. He had
achieved it. He'd done more than speak beautiful words.

Suddenly an idea flooded Jim's mind. Suppose he were to
substitute himself for Kevin . . . . ? The awesome implications
overwhelmed him. He knelt down. He worked out a concrete
plan. It would be dangerous. It would put his own life at risk.
But Kevin, Rosaleen and their children might be saved.

He would almost certainly be shot. Sweat broke out all over
his body at the prospect. To draw attention away from Kevin
he himself would have to walk into an almost certain death . . . .

He remembered Jesus' agony before his passion and felt
strangely comforted.

Jesus' death had always fascinated him.

The why of it.

Why did Jesus have to die?

He had pleaded with his Father in Gethsemani. 'Let this
chalice pass me by.'

'No', the Father had replied. *'You must die.
I want you to suffer and die so that others may live.'*

Jim found it easy to understand Jesus' love, his readiness to
sacrifice himself.

He had never been able to understand the inexorable will of
God the Father.

God had decreed pain, blood, death.

Jim stared into the darkness and shivered.

God was demanding the ultimate sacrifice from him now.
Never before had he felt so close to Jesus. There was fear in it,

stark fear, but excitement too; a thrill that was bitter and sweet at the same time.

A great calm came over him, the deep conviction that he had found the right way.

He prayed for half an hour more in wordless ecstasy. Then he went to bed and fell asleep almost instantly.

Next day he outlined his plan to Kevin.

'Tomorrow evening we will go into action. I will come here at four. We'll swap clothes. You'll put on my cassock and I will put on your clothes. We're almost of the same stature and in the dark they're bound to mistake us. I'll leave at six with a bag as if I'm carrying the explosives. That will draw any interested parties away from the house.

I'll arrange for a friend of mine to pick you up in his car: you yourself in my cassock, Rosaleen and the kids. He'll take you to Dublin. You can stay with a cousin of mine for some time till you find better accommodation. Don't bother about your things. Only take one or two suitcases with your immediate needs. I'll pack the rest and send it after you once you're safe. If you take too much now it may still attract attention. Our one concern is to get you all off to Dublin until the thing blows over.'

'That's great', Kevin stammered. 'I'll be happy to get away. But what will happen to you? These guys are as mean as snakes. They'll take it out on you from both sides once they find out.'

'Leave that to me', Jim said lightheartedly. 'I know how to deal with this. I'm made of the kind of weed that's indestructible.'

'Tell me once more the precise instructions about the drop', Jim said after a while.

Kevin closed his eyes and repeated the instructions in a

staccato voice.

'Enter Locksmith Gardens from Broadway side at half past six to seven. Come alone. If you have company we'll know you've doublecrossed us. Carry the stuff in a brown shopping bag. Walk up to Number 17, ring the doorbell twice and deposit the cargo on the doorstep, where the milkman leaves the bottles. Don't wait. Don't look back. Just walk on and out.'

'That's clear', Jim said.

'You're actually going there?!' Kevin exclaimed.

'I may have to - to give you time for your get away. But don't worry. I'm like the cat with nine lives.'

Rosaleen had tears in her eyes when they explained the gist of the plan to her.

'Thank you, Father', she said. 'You really do care.'

Jim felt strangely elated. He was doing something worthwhile . . . .

SIX

On the day itself Jim was quite busy making the various preparations. Everything was set when he arrived at the Donovans, wearing a long black cassock under a plastic mac. It was raining slightly.

Jim played with Bernie and Melanie while Rosaleen and Kevin completed their sorting and packing. At half past five Kevin and he exchanged clothes. In spite of the tension Rosaleen had to laugh at seeing Kevin in a cassock.

'Are you sure you want to go through with it?' Kevin asked Jim.

'Of course.'

'Well, here's the shopping bag. I've put two pound packets of table salt inside. It feels like the real stuff.'

'Splendid!'

'Look after yourself.'

Taking leave Jim felt emotional. He hugged the children and kissed Rosaleen on both cheeks. Giving Kevin a firm hand he imparted a final piece of advice.

'Never get yourself into the same trouble again.'

'Sure. I've learnt my lesson.'

With Kevin's coat pulled high over his neck and ears Jim went on his way. Just as well the drizzle had not subsided. It made his disguise that more difficult to detect.

Locksmith Gardens was in a Protestant area, about twenty-five minutes' walk he had calculated. It would take him to his destination just at the right time.

He had hoped his plan was working out. If all was well, anyone watching the Donovans' house was now being lured to follow him. He tried to listen for footsteps after him. Surreptitiously he looked around once or twice and imagined he saw silhouettes. But he could not be sure. Though the streets were already rather empty, there were enough people to cover a shadowing job.

The walk helped him steady his nerves. He had always been like that. In his college days Gaelic football was his favourite sport. He had often played for the college in its first team. Before a match he would be on edge, unsure of himself. But a few minutes into the game, and he would find his stride and battle on regardless of crowd pressure, fear of failure or frustrated ambition.

'Funny', he thought. 'For all I know I'm walking to my death. We were always told to prepare carefully for death. Making an act of contrition and that sort of thing. I've made no will. I've not taken leave of my family . . . . But Dad will understand and be proud of me.'

He arrived at Broadway, then turned into Locksmith Gardens.

Involuntarily he stopped, to listen and look. He understood now why this street had been chosen. It was completely deserted and only dimly lit by weak lamps on ancient wrought-iron posts.

'Once I've made the drop I'll be a perfect target', he thought. 'My only chance is to turn abruptly after leaving the packet and run for it.'

An eerie silence hung in the street as his footsteps sounded on the pavement, occasionally splashing in little pools of water. Number sixteen! He crossed the road to look for seventeen. With his heart beginning to pound in his throat, he opened the low gate of the tiny front garden, pressed the doorbell, threw the bag onto the doorstep and sprinted back.

The loud bang of a gunshot shattered the peace of the night.

He heard a bullet whizz past his head and dived for cover. Suddenly a gun battle erupted from three sides. One of the guns fell silent. A man came running across the street and jumped down flat next to Jim where he lay on the grass of the front garden. Jim recoiled with fright.

'Trust me', the man whispered. 'I'm one of your dad's friends.'

Enormous relief surged through Jim but he was given little time for celebration.

'Follow me!' the man said.

Together they ran down the street where doors and windows were beginning to be cautiously opened. They kept running through the rain down one street and up another till they reached a small alley running behind people's houses. Jim's companion entered the alley, pushed open a back gate, swung into the open kitchen and shut the door behind Jim.

Both men were panting.

'You're safe here for the time being', the man said. 'Stay in this kitchen till we come to fetch you. The people of the house are upstairs. It's better you don't meet them.'

A minute later he had gone again, leaving Jim to recover from the shock of the sudden brutal confrontation.

Two hours later Bill, the old gentleman, entered the kitchen. He gratefully accepted a cup of tea which Jim had held in readiness.

'The coast is clear. For now anyway.'

'Thanks for your timely intervention.'

'We knew you were in trouble and decided to keep an eye on you all the time. Just as well. A reception committee was waiting for you to finish you off.'

'My God!'

'You can say that again. Instead they've lost one of their best marksmen - or shall we say 'assassins'?'

Jim shuddered.

'Now first the good news. Derry, that's our commander is impressed by you, after we found out what you were trying to do. He sends you his compliments. Says you're a brave lad and an unusual priest. You're taking after your dad, he says. And he's not given to flattery, Derry isn't. He asked me to tell you that you could join our organisation in some supportive role if you care to.'

'I decline the honour', Jim said firmly.

'That's your privilege. But remember it's an open offer. You may reconsider any time.'

'Thank you.'

'Now the bad news. What do you think was in the brown shopping bag?'

'Table salt Kevin told me.'

'He cheated you. It was the real stuff.'

Disbelief showed on Jim's face.

'It teaches you not to trust anyone in this business and to check things out for yourself before committing yourself to anything. Kevin had access to the real stuff and decided to send it as added security for his family. It was a mistake. The IRA came to know. They moved in fast. Kevin's dead body was found floating down the river half an hour ago.'

'And what about Kevin's wife - and the children?'

'They're still in the house. The provos turned your car away. You better go there to break the news to the poor girl.'

At ten o'clock Jim stood once more at the door of the Donovans' apartment. He knocked. No response. He knocked louder. Again no response. He could hear the children crying inside.

'Rosaleen?' he shouted, 'It's me!'

When even this produced no results, he pushed the door firmly and found it gave way.

Utter chaos in the living room but no one to be seen.

'Rosaleen?!' he called again.

He approached the bedroom door, turned the handle and looked inside.

To his horror he saw Rosaleen's limp body hanging from the ceiling. She had been strangled with one of her own tights and strung up by the neck from the lamp shade. Bernie and Melanie sat on the bed holding her by her trouser legs.

Jim gently removed the children, hugging them. Then lowered her body and laid it out on the bed. Her face was red and blue, her features contorted in the agony she had endured.

Jim knelt next to her body and, holding Bernie and Melanie each in one arm, he wept his silent prayer of frustration.

What had gone wrong?

Why had Kevin been so stupid?

Why had they needed to kill Rosaleen too? Had she been judged an accomplice to Kevin's betrayal? Or had Gerry conveniently silenced an awkward witness? Or taken revenge on her? No one would ever know. Justice would not be done because the police could not be told the full story. And no one would give evidence.

Bitterly he reflected how Rosaleen had been right after all. She had been on her own in the end with nobody to help her. In a way she had been closer to Christ in her suffering and desolation than he had been.

And what about God? Again he had struck in an unpredictable manner. He had refused to accept Jim's sacrifice and had instead demanded that Kevin and Rosaleen pay the price. Not only Kevin who might be held responsible, but Rosaleen too.

The dark mystery of God's hardness left a cold chill in Jim's heart. Life is grim indeed if your God has a cruel streak!

There was commotion in the parish on account of Kevin's murder and Rosaleen's presumed suicide. Rumours, maliciously fed by Gerry, Jim was sure, implicated himself as partly responsible.

Jim could not defend his honour in public. He rode the storm of muted questioning and criticism by quietly looking after the business of the funerals and settling the children with relatives in Belfast and Cork.

Father Flaherty cross-examined him about the whole affair. All Jim said was that he had been consulted by Kevin and Rosaleen, that he had tried to help as well as he could and that his tongue was tied by the secret of confession. That was something Flaherty understood. He brooked no further criticism of his assistant on the part of the parishioners.

But a week later Flaherty summoned him again.

'I backed you in the parish because your lips are sealed by the secret of confession and I'm willing to accept your good intentions. But I don't want you to think all is well. I've been too long in the jungle of life not to be able to smell monkey business from a mile off. Why, I ask myself, was Kevin found dead wearing your cassock? Why did you wear his clothes when you found Rosaleen? Somewhere along the line you've been mighty stupid.'

'I did what I thought best.'

'It can't have been very good.'

'Why not?'

'Christ said: 'By their fruits you shall know them.' What have been the fruits of your interference?
Two deaths. Surely there must have been a massive miscalculation on your part.'

'God overthrows all human calculations', Jim said with some vehemence. 'The Bible says: 'God gives life and God brings death.''

Flaherty sighed. 'You're stubborn as well. If you don't mend your ways you will end up doing things as a priest that will make Christ, your Saviour, blush!'

It was a prophecy Jim would have occasion to recall.

SEVEN

A year later, when the trauma of Rosaleen's death was beginning to wear off, the ILF reared its head again with a vengeance. It happened on his mother's birthday. Jim had taken the day off to attend the celebrations in his parents' home in Belfast. More than twenty people had descended on the small house: an uncle and aunt, his brothers and sisters with their children, a couple of cousins from across the border.

Dinner was a chaotic affair since there was no space in any room to seat so many guests at once. Plates with steaming food were served in the kitchen and carried to wherever people found themselves. Jim enjoyed the banter and lighthearted gossip that forms the juice of family gatherings. His father, Noel, had been the life and soul of the party all morning, especially after he had helped himself a number of times to a generous dose of poteen. Jim had successfully avoided his company until the early afternoon. Then his father cornered him.

'Son, let's go for a walk in the park. We need to bloody talk.'

As soon as they were on their own, Noel revealed his mind. He was not the kind of man to beat about the bush.

'You owe me one for the mess I pulled you out of last autumn.'

'You pulled me out?'

'Of course me. Without me no one would have lifted a finger.'

Jim shook his head. Then relented.

'Right. I owe you one. So what?'

'D'ye know Craig prison?'

44

'Heard of it.'

'A pal of mine is there. Got nicked for possessing a gun. He's in trouble.'

'What kind of trouble?'

'The Brits are stamping on him with their boots. He knows too much. The lads think he may squeal if the screws are put on real tight.'

'Has he been sentenced?'

'No. Not yet. His case will come up in two months' time. They'll squeeze out of him what they can before then.'

'Well, they're always squeezing, aren't they? What makes you think he'll crack up?'

'His wife. She's an invalid. Lost both legs in a car crash. Depends totally on him. He'll sell his soul to Satan to get out.'

'I see.'

'I want you to go and visit him. Regular like. Once a week. Till the guards get used to the idea.'

'They won't let me in. I'm not a relative.'

'You are. I'm speaking of Hugh Mullan. He's a third degree cousin of Helen, your mother's brother Tom's wife. You haven't met the Mullans because they live in County Tyrone. But they're part of the family and you being a bloody priest and all that, they're damn sure to let you visit him.'

'They may. But what can I do?'

'To start with, cheer him up. After a while, when the screws have got used to you, you can take him messages. You'll be told what to do when the time's ripe.'

'I don't like it', Jim protested. 'The Front is just going to use me. I don't want to be a scout or a courier.'

Noel turned to him with anger in his voice.

'Whose side are you on? Can't you see this man is in trouble and we have to get through to him?'

'I'm ready to help anyone who's in need. I really am. What you're asking is different. You're trying to recruit me as a courier for your organisation.'

'And what's wrong about that? You didn't protest when we saved your life last year. You're either a bloody coward or

45

bloody stupid. Can't you get it into your head that it's only through organisations like the Front that we can help our people and defend ourselves?'

'That's alright for you, but I'm a priest. I'm called to be a man of God. We priests are not allowed to get mixed up in politics, warfare or business. We're to be free to give people spiritual help.'

'Bullshit. I never studied in a seminary but even I know that that's no more than a load of crap. Good priests have always been good Irishmen. They've been prepared to do anything to save our people from their state of misery. What's the bloody use of your being a priest if you refuse to do what any other decent Irishman would gladly do?'

Jim did not respond. His father continued.

'Our people will never be truly free and independent unless we fight for it. The bishops condemn the IRA and the ILF now, out of political convenience. Later, once Ireland is united, they'll be the first to acknowledge that our members were heroes and martyrs for the cause. Why this bloody hypocrisy? It's now we need all the support we can get.'

Jim had never won an argument with his father. Moreover, in his heart of hearts he agreed with a lot the older man was saying .... . He decided to compromise.

'Look here, Dad, I'm ready to see Hugh Mullan, whether he's a distant cousin or not. I'll do for him what I can when the time comes if I'm convinced it's right for me to do so. But tell your bosses I don't want to be a stooge at the beck and call of the Front.'

'You'd not be a stooge but a soldier', his father said, with vehemence.

'Don't let Hugh Mullan down. He's one of us. I don't mean just one of the family. I mean: one of the Irish people. Didn't Christ say you have to leave the ninety-nine sheep and save the one in trouble? Hugh's in trouble. Don't let him down.'

Hugh certainly was in trouble. Jim could see at a glance that the man was a nervous wreck. It had not proved too difficult for Jim to get a visitor's pass. Having entered through massive security doors from one guarded enclosure to the next, he was mentally prepared to meet a hardened fighter. Instead, the fifty-year old man who faced him from the other side of the grill looked frail and close to a breakdown.

'Thank you for coming to see me, Father', Hugh said. Beads of perspiration stood out on his pale forehead. His eyes darted anxiously from left to right.

'How's your health?' Jim said. He wondered how he could keep a conversation going. Both men were acutely aware of the guard behind Hugh and possible hidden listening devices.

'Not too bad. Not too bad. Have had a cold. Life's like a camping out holiday here, without the panoramic views of course. How's Theresa?'

'She's alright', Jim said guessing Hugh was referring to his wife. 'Can I give her a message from you?'

'Give her my love', Hugh said keenly. 'Tell her that I miss her a lot and hope to be back soon when all this nightmare has been cleared up. When will you see her?'

'Tomorrow', Jim improvised.

'Good. Take her some flowers from me. She likes roses, red roses. You may have to put them in a vase yourself. She can't move about that easily as you know. You'll find vases in the kitchen below the sink, behind the rubbish bin, at the back. But she could tell you that herself. She's all with it, my Theresa is, in spite of her handicap.'

'She certainly is', Jim said, to encourage him. He could have kicked himself for not having visited her before coming here.

When their time was up, Jim had warmed to Hugh. Whatever his record might be, Hugh was hardly a mindless terrorist; more a feeble and frightened man, caught up in a war beyond his emotional strength.

Visiting Theresa in Cricklewood, Co. Tyrone, was more problematic than visiting Hugh in Craig prison had been. Cricklewood was graced by public transport only once a day. Jim had to prevail on Father Flaherty to lend him his car for the day, a favour the parish priest only conceded after the pastoral necessity had been explained to him.

'Don't be taken in by that fellow Mullan looking frail and contrite', Flaherty bellowed at him. 'If he was carrying a gun, he had murder on his mind. It's easy to look frail and frightened afterwards.'

Hugh and Theresa lived in a small cottage off the main street. Holding the bunch of roses he had bought at Hugh's request he walked round to the back of the cottage and knocked on the kitchen door. No response. He tried the door. It was unlocked. He let himself in. The kitchen was in an awful state. Unwashed plates and dishes stood piled up in the sink. Bits and pieces of half eaten food lay scattered on the table and the floor. A heavy rancid smell filled the room.

Jim walked through the kitchen into the hallway. He guessed Theresa must be in the front room. He called her name and knocked on the door. Again no response. Gently he opened the door. There she was, sitting in bed propped up against a pile of pillows, her eyes wide with fright, staring at Jim as if she had seen a ghost. Although her long blond hair was unkempt, she looked quite pretty.

'Hello!' Jim said as cheerfully as he could. 'You must be Theresa. I'm Jim O'Brien. I've come to give you greetings from Hugh.'

He extended his hand to shake hers, then proffered the roses.

'These are from Hugh with lots of love.'

Theresa clasped the roses and burst into tears.

'Come on, come on', Jim said, sitting down on a chair next to her and laying his arm round her shoulder.

'Hugh's alright. Saw him yesterday. He says he's thinking of you all the time and hopes to come back soon.'

She shook her head and kept sobbing.

Whatever Jim said, she did not speak a word although she was clearly taking in whatever he was saying.

'I'll put these roses into a vase for you.'

Jim returned to the kitchen and looked for a vase in the place Hugh had indicated. He found one. While he was arranging them, someone else entered the kitchen from the back door: a young woman carrying provisions.

'I'm Stephanie O'Connor, the district nurse', she said. 'And who are you?'

'Jim O'Brien from Londonderry. I've come with news from her husband. What's wrong with Theresa? Does she never speak?'

Stephanie sighed.

'Theresa is folding up. She's had a lot of disappointments in life. No children, only miscarriages. Then, ten years ago, the accident. It took her very long to adjust to her handicap. In the end she somehow managed, mainly because Hugh was so supportive. Since his arrest, she's caved in. I'm fighting a losing battle to make her face reality. She can actually look after herself if she wants to. But she's giving up. She doesn't want to clean or wash up or do anything in the house. She's reverting to being a baby who's fed and washed and cuddled by other people. I don't know how to shake her out of it. If she continues in this way, she'll end up in an institution.'

'Does she not have relatives or neighbours who could help her?' Jim asked.

Stephanie shrugged her shoulders.

'Don't know. They're not from this area. Anyway, it might make her even more dependent. She'll have to learn to live on her own. Otherwise it's curtains . . . . '

Jim stayed around for some hours, even after the house had been cleaned up and Stephanie had had her session with Theresa.

Before he left Theresa spoke.

'You'll look after Hugh, won't you? Please, look after him. He's all I've got.'

'I will', Jim said.

Suddenly she turned to the side table, pulled open a drawer and found a bar of chocolate. She handed it to Jim.

'Give this to Hugh from me. He loves chocolate.'

She looked at him expectantly, her eyes two blue marbles in her pale frightened face.

Jim took the chocolate, bent over, kissed and hugged her and left.

He did not know what he was going to tell Hugh.

EIGHT

A few days later Jim was walking back home from taking communion to the sick when he was stopped by an elderly gentleman. It was Bill, the contact man from the ILF.

'Let's have a cup of coffee together', Bill suggested pointing at a Wimpy bar.

'How's Hugh?' Bill began as soon as they were seated.

'Not very well', Jim said and he gave a brief report on his findings.

'It confirms what we've been hearing all along', Bill commented. 'Hugh's going to crack up sooner or later.'

'Why did the ILF recruit someone like him in the first place?'

'A good question.'

Bill sipped his coffee.

'I suppose I owe an explanation to you. In the past Hugh was much more dynamic and free. His wife's accident changed all that. He still wanted to continue working for us, however, and it so happened that his services proved useful on a number of occasions. A man pushing a wheelchair can transport weapons and ammunition in a way few other people can. The problem is that through this work he got to know some sensitive links in our network. If he opens his mouth, we'll suffer some heavy setbacks.'

'You're worried about your network. Not about the man himself or his wife.'

'Of course we're concerned about Hugh, and Theresa. Incidentally, how is she? You went to see her I believe?'

'I did. You're well informed.'

'We always are.'

Jim told him what he had found in Cricklewood.

'Theresa is in a bad way', he concluded.

'They both are. What makes it worse is that their welfare is linked to the safety of many other members.'

'Including your own.'

Bill hesitated.

'Yes, including my own.'

'So what can you do about it?'

'We'll have to spring him.'

'Get him out you mean?'

'Yes.'

'Forget about it. I've seen the fortifications of the prison. The one enclosure within the other. Steel doors, thick walls, armed guards everywhere. Electronic alarms and closed circuit TV for good measure. It can't be done.'

'There are more ways of skinning a cat.'

'Meaning what?'

'We can spring Hugh when he's not in prison. And this is where you come in. On your next visit, the day after tomorrow, we want you to take him a message.'

'What message?'

'A small text.'

Bill reflected for a moment.

'Did you say Theresa asked you to take Hugh a bar of chocolate?'

'Yes.'

'Where is it?'

'Why?'

Jim hesitated, then felt in the side pocket of his jacket. 'Here it is.'

'Give it to me', Bill said.

He eyed the bar from all sides.

'That will just do fine. Leave it with me for one day. We can put a message inside in a way that will escape even close scrutiny.'

'What's the message about?'

'I shouldn't be telling you, really . . . . But since you want

52

to know and we need your help .... Well, we'll tell him to be ready during his appearance before a magistrate's court next week. We're planning a little surprise for the Brits .... '

Throughout the day Jim was troubled about the turn events were taking. Would he be doing the right thing by delivering the message to Hugh? Did it not make him an accomplice of what was considered by many, including the bishops, a terrorist organisation? He decided to consult Father Albert Murry who had been for years his spiritual adviser in the seminary.

Murry was known as a progressive moral theologian with broadminded principles. But when Jim, under the secrecy of confession, had explained his dilemma, Murry threw up his arms and raised his voice.

'Jim, Jim, what are you telling me now? You're considering giving support to terrorists? They're murderers. They kill people. They use violence. Don't you recall Pope John Paul's words at Drogheda in 1979? No good can come from a campaign that uses violence, he said. He was right.'

'But sometimes violence is needed. Like getting Hugh out of prison. I've seen the desperate situation he and his wife are in. And think of all the other people who might get hurt if Hugh gives up. Why can't I help in some small way?'

'Because by helping them, you are in fact supporting the whole organisation. You then share in all their deeds of unjust violence. You know that our bishops have repeatedly stated that it is a mortal sin for a Catholic to become or remain a member of an organisation that arrogates to itself the right to bear arms or to use them against other people or the State. You can't ignore such warnings.'

'The bishops can be wrong.'

'They can be. But not in this case. Terrorism is murder. You may not be part of it as a Catholic, and certainly not as a priest.'

'Why call it terrorism? Why not liberation? Is violence

never justified to free people from oppression?'

'Maybe in certain circumstances. We're allowed to defend ourselves against unjust aggressors. But here it's different. In our situation private groups like the ILF attack legitimate authorities.'

'Are the Brits the legitimate authorities? On what title? Haven't they occupied Ireland unjustly and oppressed our people down the centuries? What's wrong in our fighting a war against them with every means at our disposal?'

Murry sighed.

'Jim, I've heard this nationalist talk before. Of course we can fight for a fair recognition of our rights but not with every conceivable means including violence. But even, supposing - supposing the nationalist cause did allow the use of arms, you as a priest should not be part of it. You are consecrated to God. Your hands are anointed. They are sacred. Set apart for the service of God and the ministry of the sacraments. You may not use those same hands to inflict damage on other people.'

'To me it sounds like a whole lot of holy hooey', Jim replied. 'As a priest I'm consecrated to serve my people, to bring them to God. To do so I have to be totally on their side. If they are hungry, I should be hungry with them. If they suffer an epidemic, I should be there to share it with them. If they fight for their freedom, I should be part of that fight. How could I otherwise be one of them?'

'But think of the other side, the people you're fighting. The hurt and suffering you'll be causing to them. Don't they have a right to your priestly affection and concern?'

Jim reflected.

'If one's fighting, one can't help inflicting harm on one's opponents. After all, they *are* the unjust aggressors.'

'Innocent people too are made to suffer.'

'Maybe. But isn't that God's problem? He too is making innocent people suffer all the time. Think of earthquakes, floods, incurable diseases. We don't know why he does it, but he doesn't seem to care about inflicting such suffering. It's just part of human existence I suppose. So why should we care too much about it? When it's unavoidable I mean?"

'Jim, you're confused', Murry said. 'As your spiritual adviser I must tell you that you're not in a fit frame of mind to take a responsible decision. Take my advice. Don't deliver the message. Visit Hugh and Theresa by all means to give them human and spiritual support but don't let yourself be dragged into direct involvement with terrorism. I warn you it's like a spider's web. Once you're entangled you can't get out.'

Father Murry's stern words shook Jim more than he would admit to himself. They also aroused in him a surprising amount of anger and resentment. It was just as if Murry had opened a deep wound which began to disgorge a lava stream of turbulent emotions.

On the way down from Father Murry's room in the huge seminary building Jim passed the gymnasium where as a seminarian he used to do his daily work-out. He opened the door and looked in.

A dozen students stood in the far corner forming what turned out to be an impromptu boxing ring. Jim's arrival was welcomed with cheers. He was still remembered as a tough boxer during his college days.

Jim came close and saw how a third-year theologian, a certain Francis from County Kerry, a heavily built individual, was sparring against a much younger and leaner lad Jim did not know. Jim had never liked Francis and resented the obvious inequality of the duel.

Responding to the angry feelings boiling up inside him, he pushed his way into the middle of the ring and said to the junior partner, 'Give me your gloves. I'll show this lout what boxing means.'

There were cheers all round. Jim slipped off his jacket and his shoes, put on the boxing gloves and faced Francis.

'Now try your tricks on me.'

Francis hung back at first. But when Jim dealt him a couple of hard-hitting punches - to the excitement of the onlookers, he rose to the fight and gave Jim as good as he got. The result was a contest that became more vicious as time went on. Jim, who had been out of practice for some years, heaved and panted trying to keep up with the younger man. Francis spotted his discomfort, lunged forward and hit him with a left hook. The students cheered as Jim reeled under the blow.

All the pent-up anger in Jim now came to the boil. Rallying his strength, he threw himself on his opponent with fresh ferocity. His face was flushed. His vision was misted over by sweat dripping from his forehead. All he knew was that he wanted to strike, and strike again, and strike hard. Francis retreated till he stood with his back to the wall. The students shouted warnings. But Jim continued, delivering one crushing blow after the other till Francis holding both gloves before his face sank to his knees.

Jim stopped. His head spun. He looked at his gloves, then at the students who watched him in bewildered silence.

'I'm sorry', he said.

He pulled off the boxing gloves, looked around for his jacket and shoes, put them on in a daze and looked back to see Francis still sitting on the floor, pressing wet towels against the bruises on his face.

'Francis, I'm sorry', he said again. Then he turned round and walked out, aware of the hostile silence surrounding him.

Jim had always been proud of his boxing skill. 'Celts are born fighters', he used to say. This time it had been more than a game. He knew he had taken out on Francis layer upon layer of suppressed aggression: aggression against the Protestants who killed and robbed his people, against the British who protected them, against the Church authorities who were playing it safe, against his father who had never accepted him as a man, and now against Father Murry whose counsel would make him a coward.

NINE

Jim returned home from his meeting with Father Murry less than satisfied. In the past he had always made it a point to defer to the judgment of his spiritual adviser. He despised sportsmen who argue with a referee or umpire. He agreed to the old slogan that no person can be an unbiased judge in his own trial. Following the advice of his spiritual guide came naturally to him. This time he could not, and it added to his inner upheaval. His uncontrolled behaviour in the gym still rankled his nerves.

At supper he only listened halfheartedly to Father Flaherty's usual chatter. Afterwards he sat listlessly through a TV comedy that would normally have kept his attention. He wandered off to the church for his night prayers but he did not even bother to open his breviary. Something needed to be resolved. He had to take a decision, one way or the other. He sat down in a pew at the back of the church and took stock of his feelings.

In the past, he felt, other people had made decisions for him: his parents, teachers in the seminary, his spiritual director. Now he would have to take his own decision. Never mind what others might say, including the bishops. He was personally responsible to God who would judge him by his own conscience.

Once this point had been cleared, he knew what he would do. He would accept the commission entrusted to him by the ILF and deliver the bar of chocolate. That was his own decision, the one that gave him peace of mind. He knelt down and offered his resolution to God.

Entering the kitchen to make himself a cup of coffee, he looked out of the back window and noticed that the light in the bicycle shed had been left on.

He walked to the shed, opened the door and was just about to switch off the light when his gaze fell on a curious phenomenon.

At the back of the shed a spider had woven a thick web across the back window. A cross hung in the spiral threads that glistened in the reflected light. It was a St. Bridget's cross, the kind people make of a folded reed and stick up against the wall. It hung pathetically in the web, as a victim ready to be sucked empty by a hungry spider.

Jim recalled Father Murry's words. 'Don't get entangled in the web. You won't get out!' But here it was the *cross* that was entangled. It was Jesus helplessly swinging in a spiral of violence .... The symbolism struck Jim. It seemed like a sign of affirmation.

Back in his room he took out his notepad and began to write a letter. The words flowed from his pen as if they had been pent up inside him for many years and now were released for the first time.

Dear Father Murry,

I'm sorry if I lost my temper with you this afternoon. I hope I did not offend you.

I was confused this afternoon but I am no longer so now. I have decided to join hands with the ILF in the small service they have asked me to perform.

I feel I have to do this because I cannot be neutral in the struggle for the complete freedom and independence of my people. I feel in my bones the anger and frustration of all those generations of Catholics who have been cheated out of their property and their livelihood by Protestant aggressors. Christ would not have remained neutral.

I realise that I should avoid bloodshed as a priest. I assure you that I have not the least intention of being directly involved in hurting any other person. But has it not been a longstanding tradition that priests can serve as chaplains in armies? During the last world war the Germans had their Catholic chaplains and so had the Allies. These chaplains supported their armies through more than just their spiritual ministry. They carried messages, cared for the sick, cleaned trenches and at times helped ward off attacks.

Our people are engaged _in a war_. That's the central point we should recognise. It's an even more difficult war because it has to be fought underground. Our people rightly feel betrayed if bishops and priests want to play it safe and publicly support the established powers. What will history say about us in the future? We have come to despise those priests and bishops who supported the Nazi regime in Germany. Those who opposed the Nazis and ended up in concentration camps are universally regarded as heroes and martyrs. Are we not in a similar situation?

You talked a lot about violence, as if it is always wrong. I believe that violence can be God's way of producing new life. Look at Jesus. Why did the Father insist that he should suffer? Because, for some mysterious reason, God creates life out of death.

It's so easy for us, priests, to mouth mild words like peace, kindness, love and forgiveness, but will it actually undo injustice? Priests have preached their innocuous sermons for centuries without thereby liberating slaves or improving the situation of colonised peoples. It is only when social reformers began to mount violent opposition that oppressive systems began to crumble. We have to opt for deeds. Words count for nothing if we do not back them up with deeds.

I know the IRA and other nationalist groups have made mistakes. But so have the UDR, the police and the British army. Hitler made mistakes but it did not stop German Catholics fighting for their country. Whether we like it or not, these nationalist movements do represent the cause of our people.

Sometimes we read in spiritual books that it is love that will change the world. It's a fallacy. Love bonds people in friendship. It does not effect real change. Forgive me if, once more, I refer to the example of Jesus Christ. Why did the Father demand his sacrifice? Because God's sense of justice required it. God's honour had to be repaired by full satisfaction. Sins *had to be forgiven by vicarious punishment. Love may have been there as a <u>motive</u>, the change came about by the violent deed of justice.*

For all these reasons I feel talk of love as a solution is a cop-out. When I mingle with my people I want to feel inside me that I have proved my belonging to them by having acted on their behalf. I want to share in their sacrifice and their struggle. I am ready to take risks and to be blamed by those who don't understand. The one thing I don't ever want to be is a bystander - or worse someone who's made himself an outsider by joining the enemy.

I am sure God will back me up in this decision. Thank you for having given me so much of your time and, please, keep me in your prayers. I will need them now more than ever.

Yours truly in Christ,

Jim O'Brien

Even when he had gone to bed, Jim could not sleep for a long time.

He knew his letter to Father Murry was a watershed. He was committing himself to a course of action that was contrary to the official policy laid down by the Church.

'He's as stubborn as an ass!' he had once heard his mother say to his father. Jim had been seven at the time. He had been sent to bed without food because he had refused to kiss Aunt Briege who had come to see them for the day. Jim had crept down the stairs to see if he could find something to eat and overheard his parents talk in the kitchen.

'He's just like yourself', his mother had continued. 'Once he's got something in his head, you can't get it out with a sledgehammer.'

'But what's all the fuss about?', his father had grunted. 'Why can't he be nice to Briege?'

'I don't really know', his mother had said.

Jim had known.

Aunt Briege had treated him most unjustly the year before.

Jim had been playing marbles with a group from the street and a cheeky little brat named Andy had pocketed his prize marble, a green whopper, claiming it was his own. A hand-to-hand fight had ensued in which Jim was just gaining the upper hand when Aunt Briege had interfered. She had taken him by his ear and dragged him away in spite of his violent protests. He not only lost a cherished possession, but also a good deal of prestige among his peers. And, most of all, she had hurt his sense of justice. He, Jim, had been the injured party and she had effectively sided with the aggressor.

Jim had not complained to his parents; that would have gone against the family code which required everyone to sort out his own business. But he had vowed never to speak to Aunt Briege again. He would keep reminding her of the injustice she had inflicted. No pressure from the family could divert him from the implacable stand he had taken against her.

Jim wondered how much of his strong feelings was truly a question of principle. Could it be just bloody- minded, stick-in-the-mud obstinacy? But then he recalled that people were involved. 'In the end the Church always leaves us in the lurch', Teresa had said. 'The priests run away, like when Jesus died on the cross.' He did not want ever to incur that accusation. That is why he had to be bloody-minded. Perhaps God *needs* obstinate priests like myself, he thought, priests who would not betray the people for cosy theological principles.

Jim woke up next morning far from refreshed. He remembered fitful dreams in which the bar of chocolate had played a central part. The bar had suddenly increased in size when a security man at the entrance of the prison had frisked him. It had become as large and long as a cricket bat. He had been dragged before inspectors of police but the chocolate bar had melted in their hands. This gave Jim the chance to run away, down the prison corridors, the police on his heels. He had turned a corner and found himself facing a policeman who trained an automatic gun on him. The barrel of the gun was hardly six feet away and pointed at his stomach . . . . He looked up: it was Francis who grinned, enjoying his fear . . . .

Jim washed the perspiration from his face and body and dressed in a hurry. He did not have much time. He had to say Mass for the Sacred Heart nuns in Lowbridge convent that morning, at half past six. Before leaving his room he checked on the day's readings and during his ten-minute bicycle ride to the convent he thought out how he could best introduce them. He should have done this preparation on the night before but he had been too preoccupied.

He rang the bell and was admitted into the convent. He dragged the bike right inside and left it in the hallway. He was just in time. The Sisters had finished Lauds and were waiting for him to commence Mass. He entered the sacristy, vested and opened the door to the chapel. While the Sisters sang an entrance hymn, he ascended the altar, adjusted the missal and lectionary and looked at the congregation. There were twelve of them today, most of them working in the Sacred Heart Hospital as doctors, matrons or nurses.

After the liturgical greeting Jim gave his short introduction. 'In today's Gospel reading we hear how Jesus changed water into wine at Cana', he said. 'The people at the marriage feast had nothing left but water, plain, ordinary water. The same is true of our society. We are reduced to basics. We are struggling to survive. We need the wine of Christ's joy and liberation.

'The wine at Cana carried a message. The bread and wine in this Holy Eucharist carry a message because they will be changed into the real presence of Christ . . . . '

Suddenly Jim faltered. An awful thought had struck him. The bar of chocolate carried a message . . . . It too could be changed! Why had he not thought of this before? Suppose the ILF would tamper with the chocolate, put poison in, for instance, to remove Hugh before he could talk . . . ?

Jim remembered where he was. With a few brief sentences he rounded off his words. He performed Mass, feeling uneasy and distracted throughout.

Afterwards, at breakfast, Mother Superior came in.

'Father O'Brien, you don't look well', she said. 'You grew pale as if you had a dizzy spell during Mass. How are you feeling now?'

'Fine', Jim said. 'As far as I can be - this early in the morning.'

'It wouldn't matter if you go to bed in time', she countered. 'With TV and all that, people stay up far too long.'

'The interesting stuff comes on only after midnight', Jim said, to tease her.

'Oh, dearie me, don't tell me you're looking at that rubbish . . . . Anyway, here's a little parcel someone delivered for you at the front door just now. It must be really urgent for them to send it here.'

When the Sister had gone, Jim opened the slender packet. It contained nothing else than the bar of chocolate.

Jim examined it carefully. He pushed the chocolate out of the paper wrap: he could not spot any difference. He prised open the silver paper. Everything looked normal. But he knew something had been done to the bar that could bring Hugh closer to his freedom - or his execution. What was he to do?

TEN

Back in the presbytery Jim forced himself to think his options out from the beginning. On the previous occasion, he remembered, he had been taken in. He had carried explosives in the belief it was harmless table salt. 'In this kind of business you should trust no one', Bill had said afterwards. 'You must check out everything for yourself.' Jim was determined he would precisely do that.

He examined the chocolate again. Suppose a message *was* inside, where was it to be found? Or to put the question differently, if he had to hide a message in a bar of chocolate where would he put it? There were not that many options, really. The most obvious might be to write on the inside of the wrapper with invisible ink . . . . Jim scrutinised the wrapper. It was unlikely, anyway. How would an inmate in prison without chemical equipment decipher such a message?

The next possibility was something inside the chocolate. A piece of paper wrapped in a thin tube, perhaps. Yes, that would make sense . . . . But how could he test this possibility without damaging the chocolate? An X-ray? Where could he find a suitable scanner?

Jim remembered he had seen a small X-ray machine in Dobson's shoe shop on Sangler Square. It was used to put one's foot on, to see whether it fitted comfortably inside a shoe.

Twenty minutes later he was in Dobson's, trying on some new pairs of shoes and looking at the skeletons of his feet in the one pair after the other. The assistant was amused at Jim's fascination with the machine; he was too good a salesman, however, to dampen the enthusiasm of a keen customer. He did not realise that Jim was learning to work and read the instrument. Then when Jim had sent the assistant off to search for yet another size shoe, he put the bar of chocolate under the screen. His heart jumped. A tiny, tube-like line ran unmistakably through the chocolate. His conjecture had been right.

Jim heaved a sigh of relief. Bill had not lied to him. The chocolate did contain a message. All the ILF had needed to do was bore a thin hole through the chocolate, push in the tube and fill up the end.

The visitors at Craig prison were carefully searched. Jim was glad he had taken precautions. He had originally planned to carry the bar of chocolate casually in his pocket. But what if foodstuffs were forbidden? Security might confiscate it or hold it back till after the visit. In the end Jim found a perfect hiding place. The bar fitted snugly under the leather back of his breviary, a prayer book which he could be expected as a priest to have with him.

The security guard interrogated him, examined the permit, frisked him and searched his briefcase. He opened the breviary but did not spot the chocolate at the back. Jim was through. Another guard escorted him to the room where the meeting was to take place.

Hugh looked even more miserable than on the previous occasion. Jim tried to cheer him up by talking about Theresa.

'How is she?' Hugh wanted to know.

'A bit depressed', Jim said. 'She misses you a lot. She's struggling to cope.'

'Did you take the roses?'

'I did. She loved them.'

'Thanks.'

'She sends you many greetings.' Saying this Jim slipped the bar of chocolate from his breviary and pushed it unobtrusively in Hugh's direction through the grill. Hugh took it with hardly any movement of his arm. It disappeared out of view into his sleeve.

'A social worker called Stephanie O'Connor comes in a few times a week to help Theresa', Jim continued. 'She buys supplies and helps Theresa in the house.'

'I know her.'

'She's a nice kid.'

'Sure is.'

While this conversation was going on, Jim still had the breviary in his hand. From between its pages he pulled out a slip of paper which he held in such a way that Hugh could read the words written on it. It said: MESSAGE ONLY DON'T EAT. Jim had decided to add this warning on the off chance the chocolate had been poisoned all the same. Hugh looked at Jim and nodded to signal he had understood.

They talked on, more freely now. Hugh described the daily routine in prison with a mixture of humour and bitterness. He was kept in isolation for most of the day. 'A perfect place for Carthusian monks with a perpetual vow of silence', he said. 'The screws keep me from other people. They hope I'll talk to them.'

When the guard indicated time was up, Jim took leave, giving Hugh the thumbs-up sign.

'Don't give up!'

He hoped with all his heart that the escape plan would succeed.

A few days later, at lunch, Jim received a call from the prison authorities.

'Father Jim O'Brien?'

'Yes.'

'We're contacting you with reference to Hugh Mullan.

'What about him?'

'He's suddenly taken very ill. We want to inform the family. We believe his wife is handicapped . . . . We thought you might be the best person to tell her and others.'

'What happened to him?'

'We don't know. It looks like some kind of food poisoning . . . . He's been taken to the Sacred Heart Hospital and is in intensive care. If you identify yourself to the officer on duty, he will allow you and other members of the family to talk to him, provided the Hospital allows visitors . . . . '

'Thank you', Jim said.

Thousands of thoughts came flooding into his mind. Food poisoning? Could it have been the bar of chocolate? He gnashed his teeth. How to tell Theresa and the rest of the family?

He decided the best for him was to go to Hospital first and see for himself.

Being no stranger in the Sacred Heart Hospital, he was conducted straight to the room where Hugh had been taken. The policeman in front of the door asked his name, then let him pass.

Hugh lay in bed, pallid as death itself. He wore an oxygen mask. Wires, attached to various parts of his body, led to an intensive care monitor manned by a nurse. Hugh's eyes were closed. He breathed slowly and erratically.

Jim greeted the nurse, then sat down next to Hugh. Taking him by the hand, he said gently: 'Hugh, it's me.'

Hugh opened his eyes. There was a flicker of recognition. Then he closed his eyes again.

'How're you feeling?'

Hugh shook his head.

'Hugh, I'm going to give you absolution and the anointing of the sick.'

Hugh nodded.

Jim knelt next to the bed and said an act of contrition in Hugh's hearing. Then he gave him the absolution. Standing up again, he prepared for the anointing. He had brought the holy oils with him. Holding the ritual in his left hand, he read the prayers, anointing Hugh on his palms and forehead with the thumb of his right hand.

67

Hugh was breathing heavily all the time.

'What can I do for you?' Jim said, holding him once more by the hand when the rite was finished. 'Do you want me to bring Theresa?'

Hugh opened his eyes and shook his head. Large drops of tears began to roll down his face.

'Who do you want to see?'

Again Hugh shook his head.

The nurse approached gently and whispered to Jim: 'Father, you'd better leave him for a while. He's getting upset. I can see it on the monitor.'

'I'll be back soon', Jim told Hugh.

Once outside, Jim looked for the attending doctor and got an ambivalent report.

'Mr. Mullan is in a very serious condition. His heart is slowly failing and we don't know why. We pumped his stomach empty but haven't identified any toxic substance. We're still analysing blood samples but until we know the cause there's little we can do.'

Jim was virtually certain that the chocolate he had taken to Hugh had, after all, contained poison. Utter disgust and a deep anger began to take hold of him. The ILF had used him to execute one of their own members! He thought of Theresa, the anguish Hugh's death would cause her, how it would condemn her to despair and dependency for the rest of her life! But still it was not too late. If he could trace the poison, the doctors might find the cure.

There was no way he could contact Bill. He had to ring his father.

From a pay phone in the hospital lobby he called Container Cargo Limited at Belfast.

'I want to speak to Noel O'Brien. I'm calling from the Sacred Heart Hospital in Londonderry. A cousin of his is dying.'

'Can't it wait till five?'

'It can't.'

Five minutes later his father's voice rent the silence with its usual boom.

'Who are you?'

'I'm Jim.'

'Who the hell is dying?'

'Hugh Mullan.'

'My God!' There was a stunned silence. Then his father bellowed again. 'What's happened to him? An accident?'

'Sort of. Can't talk. I have to get through to you know who.'

'I see. Trouble, hey? Alright. Where are you?'

'In the Sacred Heart Hospital in Derry.'

'Alright. Stay put. Bill will ring you in ten minutes or so. If he's at home.'

Jim waited at reception for twenty minutes till the call came. He recognised Bill's voice.

'Don't talk. Meet me where we met last. Make sure you don't have a tail.'

ELEVEN

After making a number of phone calls to Hugh's closest relatives, Jim set out for the Wimpy bar where he had met Bill last. He was determined to find out whether the ILF had poisoned the chocolate, and, if so, what poison they had used.

Bill had warned him about a tail. Jim thought a shadow would be easy to detect as he was travelling on a bicycle. He looked around as he rode off from the hospital parking area: nobody seemed to take the slightest notice. He turned into Antrim Road in the direction of the city. A yellow Renault turned into the road after him, passed and went on ahead. Had he not seen the car in the parking lot? But then, there had been so many . . . .He cycled on following the bend of the road. After half a mile he saw the yellow Renault again, parked outside a newsagent. Was it a coincidence? How could he make sure?

He remembered having read in books that driving round blocks of houses in circles or making the letter eight round two blocks exposes a shadow. He turned left into a small side street, cycled as fast as he could, turned left again at the second crossing, turned left a third time, crossed the road he had been on a few minutes before, then turned abruptly to the right.

He had been so busy scanning the street he was crossing and looking behind him that he failed to notice a van backing out of a garage. He ran into it, lost his balance and fell to the ground. Fortunately, he had not hurt himself too badly. He scrambled to his feet with the help of the anxious driver who had jumped out of the van.

'Sorry, Father. You were on top of me before I saw you.'

'Never mind. It's my fault. I was distracted.'

70

Jim picked up his bike and inspected the damage. His front wheel was slightly twisted, the lamp had been smashed. And a tiny aluminium box protruded from the springs under his saddle . . . .

It was something he had never seen. He loosened the box, held it between index and thumb and looked at it. It was perfectly round, like an old-fashioned type-ribbon box. On the underside it carried a metal rim - a magnet! Suddenly it dawned on Jim that this was an electronic tailing device which someone had fastened to the steel bar under his saddle . . . .

On impulse he put the device back where it had been, straightened the wheel between his knees, got on the bike and continued his journey.

He *was* being followed. Why? By whom? It had to be British security. Perhaps they were suspicious about a connection between his visit to Hugh and the poison attack. The last thing he could afford to do was to lead them to Bill. He should make them think he had not noticed the device.

Jim returned to the presbytery. Bill would understand what had happened when he did not turn up. He would surely take up contact in his own way.

Three hours later Jim was still anxiously waiting in the presbytery when he was called to the phone. It was the assistant administrator of the Sacred Heart Hospital

'I believe you gave the last rites to Mr. Mullan, Father.'

'Yes, I did.'

'He died a few minutes ago.'

'So soon?!'

'Yes. Terribly soon.'

'Did Philip his brother come in time?'

'I don't think so. Apart from you, no one else has been to see him. Nor will they be able to see him now. Because it is such an unusual case, we have to act with extreme caution. Since we do not know the cause of the disease there is the possibility of its affecting other inmates of Craig prison. The prison authorities have released the body to us. Our pathological department will start a post-mortem examination later today. The body will be with us till the day after tomorrow. I'm telling you this in connection with any funeral arrangements.'

Hugh's death shocked Jim profoundly. His feelings of guilt regarding the chocolate were augmented by remorse about not having acted more decisively in tracing the poison. He felt helpless, angry, defeated. Had he not given his services with the best of intentions? Why then should others have used him as an executioner?

Putting such thoughts out of his mind for the moment Jim set about informing Hugh's not-really- interested relatives of the latest developments.

That evening in church, on his knees before the high altar and the giant crucifix, Jim poured out his heart.

'God, I can't understand you.

'If you're a God of life, why do you find pleasure in death?

'Rosaleen turned to me in her need. I tried to help as well as I could - you know it, God - but you killed her. I even offered myself instead. You made me live and wanted her dead.

'Hugh was in trouble and so is Theresa. I wanted to help them. I went against the advice of my spiritual director because I cared for Hugh and Theresa and for all my people who suffer so much. You made me an instrument of his death.

'Why?

'Why did you want your son, Jesus, to die?

'He was the holiest, gentlest, most loving human being who ever lived.

'You decreed he should suffer and die.

'Why?

'Was he not 'the Son in whom you were well pleased'?

'Did you make him feel pain because you love him?

'Is this the reason why we Catholics who belong to your one

true Church, have to suffer? Because you love us?

'I can't understand you.

'But whatever you do, please, don't ever again make me the instrument of death for my own people.'

For a long time he stayed on his knees in silence. He looked at Jesus on the cross. He knew the key to the mystery of death was hidden in that crucified figure. He imagined what Jesus would say to him.

'Jim, do not despair.

'Look at me. I died but I rose again.

'Life comes through death.

'Rosaleen died. Hugh died. Many of your people die. But it has a purpose. Eventually it will lead to new life, to liberation and resurrection.

'You are right in what you did for Rosaleen and Hugh. You were on their side in their suffering. You shared in their death. One day you will be counted among those who brought new life the hard way - by sharing in suffering and death.

'Do not give up, Jim! Do not despair!'

Jim wished he could argue with Christ, ask him about the ILF.

'Have I been right in trusting them? How can I ever fight for my people if our nationalist organisations do what they like, using me and cheating me? How can I ever trust them again?'

But Jesus gave no answer.

Hugh's funeral was an extremely dismal affair, tragic beyond description. Jim conducted the service in the small parish church in Cricklewood. Some of the local people turned up; only a handful of Hugh's relatives. All were disappointed when they found out they could not see the dead man. The pathologists had sealed the coffin for health safety reasons.

Theresa attended the Mass in a state of shock. Although Jim and others had talked to her, Jim doubted whether she had grasped it was Hugh who was being buried. In his sermon and prayers Jim addressed his words mainly to her, hoping she would glean some small comfort from the ritual.

Theresa did not follow the small funeral procession to the graveyard. There was no display of paramilitary honours, almost to the disappointment of the small band of security men watching proceedings from a distance. It chilled Jim to the bone. The ILF had callously renounced Hugh's membership, disregarding his years of risky and faithful service . . . .

It was Jim himself who took Theresa home in her wheelchair. When the few relatives had come and gone, he helped her into bed and made her supper.

She looked at him with her large, blue eyes.

'When will Hugh come back?'

He remembered her previous pleas to him. 'Look after Hugh. He's all I've got.'

He could not find words to speak to her.

He sat down, held her with both hands and wept.

Two months later Jim was walking on the pavement of Bishop Street on his way back from religious instruction classes, when a dark blue Ford drew up beside him.

'Hop in, Father', a voice said. It was Bill who was sitting next to the driver.

Jim turned away angrily, but Bill called out again.

'Come on, don't cause a scene. We need to talk.'

The back door swung open. Jim reconsidered and stepped into the car. It slid away and gathered speed.

'We owe you thanks', Bill began. 'You've done your job splendidly both by taking the message into Craig prison and by not trying to meet me on that day.'

'Can we talk freely?', Jim said.

'You can. The driver is one of ours. Call him Robert.'

The driver smiled at him. It increased Jim's anger.

'I've waited for this opportunity to talk to you. You're the filthiest, meanest, lousiest, most despicable lot I've ever met. Hugh may not have been a hero and a martyr. But he was one of you and worked for you. You killed him and even disowned him at his funeral. You lied to me and cheated me, involving me in an execution without my knowing. I won't ever want to have anything to do with you.'

'Didn't I tell you he's got his father's temper', Bill said to Robert. Both men laughed.

'Let me out', Jim said. 'You make me sick.'

'Be patient, young man', Bill countered. 'We want you to meet someone.'

'I don't want to meet anyone', Jim shouted. 'Let me out!'

Bill and Robert disregarded his demand. The car sped on its way out of town, turned into a small country lane and stopped outside a farmhouse.

'I'm not going in', Jim declared.

'I saved your life once', Bill retorted. 'Trust me.'

His face flushed with anger, Jim left the car and followed the man inside.

In the spacious kitchen Jim met the farmer and his wife - and a middle aged man with sideburns, a small beard and dark-rimmed spectacles.

'A friend of yours!' Bill announced.

Jim looked more closely. Suddenly recognition hit him.

'Hugh! It's Hugh!'

'It's me!' Hugh affirmed.

'How is it possible?' Jim exclaimed. He embraced him, hugged him, danced him round the room. Both men laughed and wept, the others looking on with amusement.

When they sat down to a cup of tea, Jim asked again: 'How is it possible? What happened? Man, I buried you!'

'I can't tell you all the details', Bill began to explain. 'In short it comes to this. The chocolate contained a rare South

American poison that causes the symptoms of heart failure. The message instructed Hugh when to take the dose. It was risky, I tell you. We'd almost given Hugh an overdose. We rightly surmised the prison authorities would send Hugh to the Sacred Heart Hospital because it specialises in food poisoning. There we had allies waiting for him. After you had anointed him, the acting doctor gave Hugh a further injection that practically paralysed him so that two other doctors could concur in declaring him dead. Hugh was then moved to the pathological department where another body was substituted for him. The postmortem was done on the wrong body without the police surgeon being aware of it. Anyway, the rest was easy. We brought Hugh here to recover.'

'Marvellous' Jim said. 'Sorry for all the abuse I hurled at you.'

'Don't worry. In your place I would have said the same.'

'Does Theresa know?'

'Not yet. Tomorrow Hugh travels to the States under a new identity. After a few months we take Theresa there to join him.'

'Marvellous', Jim said again. 'It's like the end of a fairy tale.'

When Bill and Robert drove Jim back to Bishop Street, Bill had a final word.

'Derry, the big boss, had something in mind when he wanted you to meet Hugh', he said. 'We're still interested in your joining us. You're just the kind of man who can help us with unusual services, as you did for Hugh. Why don't you become a full member?'

'Give me time to think', Jim answered. 'I don't want to stand on the sidelines, but . . . . I . . . . Anyway, if you're in real trouble . . . . , if there's a real emergency, you can rely on me.'

On the 15th of August that year, the feast of the Assumption of Our Lady, Jim celebrated the ten o'clock Mass vested in black vestments.

'You may wonder why I'm standing before you wearing the chasuble of mourning', he told a packed congregation. 'I mourn the freedom of my people. On this very day, six years ago in 1969, British troops occupied my home town Belfast . . . .'

Father Flaherty was furious when he heard about it. He summoned Jim to his study.

'What the hell are you up to? Isn't the mayhem on the streets bad enough that you have to take it into church? You've disobeyed the Bishop and disgraced Our Lady!'

'It was a spontaneous act of mourning. I acted on the spur of the moment. Our Lady will understand.'

'Rubbish! You're inciting trouble. I told you before: stay out of the political wrangle or it will destroy you as a priest. With your impetuous and stubborn temper, one day you'll put your foot into it so deeply that you're in the slime for ever. I warn you: it will finish you as a minister of Christ!'

TWELVE

Twelve years and three pastoral promotions later, away from Ireland, in Frankfurt, Jim remembered Flaherty's prophetic words. 'One day you'll put your foot in so deeply you can't get out!' He had not thought then he would ever find himself in such a mess.

Jim did not fancy nightclubs. Certainly not German ones like Frankfurt's 'Ewige Eros', the slick drink, food and sex oasis he found himself in now.

He shifted uneasily in his seat as he surveyed, once again, the dimly lit lounge around him. His gaze took in the small clusters of people filling the oval shaped room - mostly businessmen with female companions of all sorts.

No one here, he hoped, knew his true identity as a Catholic priest: who now under the code name Jim O'Toole served also as lieutenant in the Irish Liberation Front.

'Relax', Paddy gestured from across the table. Young and carefree, Paddy was enjoying himself. Having downed his fifth glass of champagne he held his arm anchored round the waist of the tall blonde whose German babble he did not bother to understand.

Jim knew he could not afford to relax.

Frankfurt is not that far from Belfast. If they had made even a small mistake, a whole platoon of the LL, the 'Loyalist League', would by now be combing the city for them. And so might MI6.

He looked again. Everyone's attention was riveted on a juggler in the centre space. The man was balancing a tower of cups and saucers on top of his head, and kept adding to the pile by picking up one more cup or saucer with his foot, kicking it up into the air, then deftly moving his head with its load underneath. Jim deliberately closed his mind to these acrobatics and to the smoke, the noise, the laughter and the applause. He was studying faces.

By now he knew most. He checked them off one by one as definitely German; or, anyway, probably harmless. You are never sure, of course. Even whores might have been enlisted to look out for them. But he was willing to grant them the benefit of the doubt.

Only a few people gave cause for real concern. Once or twice he had intercepted the inquisitive look of a tall, cadaverous individual sitting next to an equally tall and lean woman a few table away. Why did the man stare? What was the interest? Also, two young men in dark suits had just entered and were standing in a corner. They seemed to be scanning the place as if they were searching for someone.

One of the two men looked in his direction. Their gaze seemed to lock, for an instant. The man looked away.

Jim shifted again in his seat. He lifted his glass and pretended to drink. From the corner of his eye he glanced at the two men once more. They were leaving the room. Jim heaved a sigh of relief.

But was his relief justified?

Suppose they *had* been the LL and had recognised them? All they would need to do now was guard the exits and close the trap. Paddy and he might be safe as long as they stayed in, they would become an easy target once they stepped into the darkness outside.

How could he be sure?

If they were the enemy, or look-outs enlisted by the enemy, their actions were predictable. The two men would split up. One would go out and post himself opposite the entrance. The other would phone for reinforcements. As soon as these arrived, or were on the way, the second man would make his way back into the lounge to keep the quarry under direct surveillance.

Sure enough, five minutes later, one of the men returned

and took his place at a table.

Jim clenched his fist. They would need to move and move fast, before more of them would arrive and seal the place up. He leant over to Paddy.

'We've been spotted.'

'How do ye know?'

'There's a fellow at the back watching us. His mate has gone out. Probably organising a reception for us at the front door. We have to get going before they're here in strength.'

'You're bloody joking.'

'I'm not.'

'What d'you want me to do? Go up to him and lay him out?'

'No. Of course not.'

Paddy could only think like a rhino, especially when he was half drunk.

'I want you to go to the gents. It's next to the bar. We'll probably find another exit, at the back. You go now. I'll follow you in two minutes.'

Paddy scowled.

'What's the hurry? You've got butterflies in your brain or in your belly.'

'Shut up! We'll move. Get going.. It's an order.'

Paddy pulled a face, shrugged himself free from the girl and, without more ado, walked in a leisurely way to the toilet.

Jim watched the mystery man at the back look up. His eyes seemed to follow Paddy's movements. It was the confirmation he had waited for.

Jim dug into his wallet and slipped the German blond two banknotes under the table. He gestured with his hand for her to stay.

'There! We come back. Stay here!' he urged.

Her remaining at the table might give a few extra seconds' respite.

The juggler had meanwhile started a new act. He had made his topless assistant stand on her head on top of a low stool. She had spread her arms and her legs. The juggler began to throw hoops, ringing her arms, her legs and even her breasts in rapid succession. People shouted in approval.

Jim stood up. The juggler was working to a climax and few paid attention to Jim's departure. He walked quickly to the toilet and glanced over his shoulder before opening the door. The man at the back had noticed. He stood up, unresolved it seemed, on what to do, then walked to the exit.

Paddy was waiting for Jim in the washroom, still sulking. They were alone.

'There's no doubt about it,' Jim blurted out. 'He's gone to tell the others that we're quitting. Any chance of getting out through here?'

'No', Paddy said. 'It's like the loos in Maze prison.'

'OK. There's a door behind the bar which leads to a kitchen, we'll try our luck there.'

They walked out, turned to the bar, pushed the bar man aside and opened the door behind him. Two waiters in the kitchen were drinking a cup of coffee. Jim and Paddy ignored them, ran through to the back, found a door leading into a small corridor, switched on the light, ran to the end of the corridor and found an outside door. It was locked, but they found the key on the overhead ledge.

Jim opened the door and looked outside. He saw a dark and narrow alley. It seemed deserted. They went out locking the door behind them.

When their eyes had grown accustomed to the dark, they began to understand the situation they were in. The alley-way, hardly ten feet wide, was flanked on both sides by sheer brick walls belonging to tall buildings. Scaling them was out of the question. They turned left, away from the main entrance. It was no good, the alley proved to have a cul-de-sac. At this end it was closed off by an iron gate that barred access to a small courtyard. There was only one way out.

Walking as close to the walls as they could, they retraced their steps and approached the corner where the alley joined the main road.

Paddy, now completely sober, inched ahead and looked

round the corner into the street. Minutes later he reported.

'The front door of the nightclub is about twenty yards to the right. There's a hitman posted outside.'

'Only one?'

'Just the one.'

'Where?'

'Round the corner with his back turned to us.'

'Can we give him the slip?'

'Not bloody likely. He'd hear us and mow us down.'

'What d'you want to do?'

'Jump him from the back. Knock him out.'

There was little choice. Jim nodded.

'OK. But don't give him more than is needed.'

Paddy shrugged his shoulders. He tiptoed back to the opening of the alley. Jim followed him closely. Paddy looked round the corner - and moved out. Jim could not help admiring him, even though he considered Paddy a brute. Muscular, tall and heavily-built Paddy walked with the agility of a bear.

In one or two strides he was close. He dealt the man a karate chop on the head, then grabbed him by the throat with his powerful big hands and dragged him backwards into the alley.

It had only taken a few seconds. They had not been seen. Paddy by now knelt on top of the man who was gasping for breath. With one hand he released his grip and searched for a gun. He found it and passed it on to Jim.

'Who are you, for Chrissake?' Paddy hissed, lifting the man's head and knocking it on the cobblestones.

The man groaned.

They heard banging on the side door in the alley. Someone was trying to force the door.

'Come on, hurry,' Jim urged. 'Leave him. We've got to get away.'

'Just a souvenir,' Paddy said. 'He's got to remember.'

With an intensity of hatred that made Jim squirm, Paddy raised his right fist and slammed it into the man's face, cracking the bones and crushing the flesh. Again and again his fist rose and came down as a sledge hammer, crunching on impact. The man twisted and turned in agony.

Jim went over and took Paddy by the shoulders to wrench him loose. Paddy got up, gave his victim who had gone limp, a final kick and ran off with Jim into the main street.

At this time of night the streets were almost deserted. They walked a long distance, zigzagging from one side street to the other, till they were sure they were not being followed.

They reached their hide-out at half past two.

Lying in bed Jim thought of all the events that had happened in the past week. He had never thought it would make him do the things he had done. But wasn't that the price of freedom? God, what would the people in his parish say if they knew what he was involved in? Sometimes he wished that he had not got mixed up in this horrible mess, then he reminded himself of his special call.

He cringed when he thought of the man in the alley-way. He heard the dull thuds of the crunching blows, the gasping and groaning . . . . Paddy could be so beastly. The man probably had children too, and a wife. Jim felt sorry for them, in spite of his dislike for the LL.

Another scene swam before his eyes: the execution of Peter Bowyer . . . . How had he suddenly got involved in such violent bloodshed? Peter's death too had been sickeningly brutal.

Perhaps, Paddy was right. He was too soft, not tough enough for this kind of warfare.

Paddy stuck his head round the door.

'May I kiss Daddy good night?'

'Get lost', Jim growled.

Next morning Sean was furious.

'You had strict instructions to hole up here for three months. You've blown your cover.'

'What else could we do?' Paddy protested. 'The bastards were after us.'

'If you'd just scarpered, the police would have stayed out. Now they're after you for murder.'

'Murder?'

'Yes, murder. It's all over the German press. They're still trying to establish the man's identity. When they do, they'll know it's us who did him in.'

'Who was he?' Jim asked softly.

'I've no idea and I couldn't care less. What worries me is that this mate of yours walked right through town, blood dripping from his hands and his shirt, leaving a trail that ends up here.'

'We were not being followed.'

'The police will have descriptions of you from people in the nightclub. Others will have seen you outside, the taxi driver, or God-knows-who-else. They'll piece together the details. Next thing we know, they'll be on our doorstep. No, you've blown our cover. We're closing the place down.'

'It's as serious as that?'

'Yes. I talked to Derry this morning. In emergencies I ring, using code. I've got instructions to ship both of you off to India. And good riddance it will be.

'India?'

'Indeed, India. We've got some friends in a hole called Hyderabad. Nobody will look for you there. I've been told to convey this message to you: 'Lie low and keep your nose clean.' You know what that means. Under no circumstances draw attention to yourself. Just stay put and do what other tourists do.'

Both men were silent for some time. Then Jim spoke up.

84

'Will my wife know where I am?'

'No. And don't try to get in touch with her. Phone calls can be tapped, intercepted. High Command will let her know you're alright. Derry doesn't want you to be smart. You'd regret it.'

Jim nodded. *Reference to the wife was the code Derry employed when speaking of his bishop. Jim had explained his hurried departure from Ireland to diocesan officials as a visit to a dying relative in the States. Emergency leave had been granted. Derry would send faked messages from Chicago.*

'When do we leave?' Paddy asked.

'This afternoon. I'm getting two new passports for you. You'll be taken by car to Zurich. From there you'll fly to Bombay.'

THIRTEEN

Queuing at the Air India counter in the large departure hall of Zurich airport, Jim was addressed by a young woman.

'Could you help me carry this suitcase?'

Jim obliged. He lifted her case, told Paddy he would be back in a minute and walked after the woman who was herself dragging another case on wheels.

She walked to the lift. Once inside, she turned to him and said: 'My name is Sue. Bill has come to talk to you. Even Sean shouldn't know we're here. There's a little coffee bar on the top floor where he's waiting for you.'

Jim found it. It was a self-service place. Bill had already captured a table and provided himself with two glasses of beer. He offered one to Jim. 'Time is short. Derry says you're upset.'

'Of course, I'm upset. I was sent to get information. Instead I find myself involved in bloody murder! I'd never have taken the job if I knew Derry would take that line.'

'Keep your voice down!' Bill said. 'Why not tell me precisely what happened. I got the gist from Derry, but I'd like to hear the details from you.'

'Why?'

'There have been some complications . . . . We're trying to spot a leak.'

Jim swallowed. He had told the story twice before and found even the telling of it quite an ordeal.

'Alright. Well, you know the first phase of the operation. As chaplain of Loch Mann detention centre I got to know its governor, Peter Bowyer, on a personal basis. As planned, last Monday night I waited for him at the corner of Dumbarton

86

Road and Plumm Road, where he parks his car. I asked him if I could see him on some private business. 'Why not?' he said. Then, as we'd foreseen, he asked me into his bachelor apartment which is just round the corner.

'There's a soldier stationed at the front of the house. Peter waved at him, said I was OK and both of us entered. He took me to his sitting room. He offered me a cup of coffee which he went to make in the kitchen. Meanwhile I located the word processor on his desk which was the real objective of the exercise.

'This was the moment when the diversionary phone call was to take place. The phone actually rang. Peter took the call and our plan seemed to work. 'That was one of my colleagues calling from the office,' he said. 'She lives two floors up. She thinks she may have forgotten to switch off her oven. Excuse me for a few minutes. I'll go up and check.'

'As soon as he'd left, I got the word processor going. On account of the good briefing I'd received, I got easily enough into the data base we wanted. I typed in the code, slipped the floppy disk I had brought with me into the machine and began to copy the data. Then he returned.

'I don't know what went wrong. He was back in two minutes, not seven as we had reckoned.

'I heard his footsteps which gave me time to move away from the word processor. But I couldn't take out the floppy disk. We began to talk, drinking our coffee. Then he noticed the word processor had been uncovered. He walked over and saw the floppy disk protruding from the slot. I knew our ploy had been detected. I had to act fast. I grabbed a heavy book from the desk and hit him over the head with it while he still had his back to me. It knocked him out.

'I wondered what to do. It looked as if the whole operation had misfired. The data would only be of use to us if they didn't know we had a copy. So I made a brief phone call to operations' control, as had been agreed in emergencies.

'They told me to sit tight. Peter regained consciousness so I tied him to a chair.

'It lasted about an hour before Paddy came on to the scene.

"What are we going to do?' I asked.

"We have to drug him and put him to bed', he said. 'A new invention. It's an amnesia-inducing drug that wipes out every recollection of the past twenty-four hours.'

'I heaved a sigh of relief, I tell you. Paddy doped him with some chloroform and I helped him drag Peter upstairs. We put on his pyjamas and made him lie in bed. Then Paddy asked me to clean up downstairs and remove traces of my presence, while he would do the same in the bedroom.

'I did as I was told. A few minutes later I heard two muffled gunshots. I ran up. I found Paddy had killed Peter: shot him straight through the blanket. It was a ghastly sight.

"Why did you do that?!' I asked Paddy.

"He woke up and attacked me', he replied.

'I knew it was a lie. I realised then that Paddy had been specifically sent to execute Peter. The more I think about it, the more I resent it. Why did he need to be killed? I would never have taken part if I'd known it would end in an execution.'

'You disappoint me', Bill said. 'The execution was not part of the original plan, as you well know. We needed the contents of the disk without any one suspecting we had a copy. No harm would have come to Peter, if you'd got away with it. The moment he found out, we had to kill him.'

'Why?'

'To protect you.'

'To protect me? In the worst case I would have been convicted of robbery. I might have got a sentence. I'd prefer that a thousand times to killing a man.'

'I'm sorry but that's sentimental nonsense', Bill said. 'Forgive me for being so blunt but I believe some plain talk is in order. First of all, *you* didn't kill him, we did. That's why we didn't ask you to do it. We sent Paddy. Secondly, you yourself knocked Peter out. You would have been convicted of assault as well as robbery. Thirdly, when I spoke of protecting you I didn't think of your comfort. As a priest you're a valuable asset

88

to us. It's in our interest to protect your cover so that you can assist us again in the future. Finally - and I'm sorry I have to say this - , stop playing the innocent. You're not stupid. You know the score. You knew we had no other option. This is war, not a game.' Jim looked at him in silence.

'Now the business of the guard', Bill resumed.

'I thought Paddy killed him too?'

'He tried to. Paddy had to work fast and did not finish the job. He had to get past the soldier before joining you. Following instructions he came on his motorbike, skidded round the corner, crashed into a sidewall and fell off. The soldier came running over to help. Paddy turned on him, stabbed him and dragged him into a ditch nearby where he would not be immediately noticed. By that time lights had gone on in neighbouring houses, so Paddy got on his motorbike again and drove off. Only half an hour later could he approach the house in safety.'

'And the soldier was still alive?'

'Exactly. He was found in the morning, severely wounded but not dead. He's recovering in hospital. That's why we want to be sure about one thing: does the soldier know you were a priest? Did you wear a collar? Did Peter call you 'Father' in his presence?'

Jim reflected.

'I don't think so. I was wearing a poloneck shirt, and grey trousers under my coat. When we passed the soldier, Peter just said 'He's alright'.'

'But you're not absolutely sure?'

'Ninety-nine per cent.'

'That's not good enough. We must be absolutely certain. Once he starts talking police may have descriptions of both Paddy and yourself. Moreover, we are convinced that Maurice Bowyer, Peter's brother who runs a central heating company in Belfast, is, in fact, the head of the Loyalist League. Put the two things together and it is clear neither of you should be around for questioning.'

After a pause Jim said: 'Talking of Peter Bowyer's family, do you know anything about a daughter of his called Evelyn?'

'No. We didn't even know he'd been married. What about her?'

'Nothing important -- he mentioned her to me.'

'Another question concerns your parish. You returned to Connaughtmarton?'

'Yes. I returned straight from Peter's house. I don't believe anyone saw me. I entered the presbytery through the back door. I'm sure Helena, that's my housekeeper, will swear I was at home all that night .... How long are we to cool off in India?'

'Approximately three months we reckon. You'll be really safe there. That is, if you don't do anything stupid. There has been a leak. We still don't know how it is that the LL could be on your trail in Frankfurt so soon.'

'You'll keep my bishop happy?'

'Yes, we will.'

'You remember, when I made my deal with the ILF, I made it quite clear that my involvement should not be at the expense of my priestly ministry. I've been called to be a priest and I want to remain a priest.'

'We know, Father', Bill said, with a trace of sarcasm.

'Remind Derry of it.'

'I will. We'll honour our part of the agreement, if you stick to yours.'

'That's a deal.'

'Derry and I and all of us in the council loved and respected your father. We wouldn't let you down, if for no other reason than for his sake.'

'Thank you.'

'The person to meet you in Hyderabad will be eating grapes. And, by the way, use Paddy's brawn but don't trust his brain.'

Sean and Paddy scolded Jim when he returned to the departure hall.

'What could I do? The stupid lass went ahead in a lift and I

90

lost her. I thought she'd planted a bomb on me so I looked inside the case. It contained women's dresses. Then she turned up, kissed me and invited me for a drink.'

They had to run to catch the plane.

The flight to Bombay took ten hours. It gave Jim time to consider his position.

When he had offered his services to the ILF he had stipulated that he did not want to be directly involved in any killing. 'I'm not a soldier. I'm a priest and want no blood on my hands', he had said. Things had worked out differently. He had been instrumental in the execution of Peter Bowyer. He had not been able to stop Paddy battering his victim to death outside the nightclub. He knew he was guilty, as an accomplice.

Had he not always known it could come to this? By associating himself with people who kill, he had, in principle, shared in their killings. He had even, on occasion, taken part in a secret shooting practice . . . . He had pacified his conscience with the thought that his attendance was purely a means to secure him the rank of lieutenant. This, he had told himself, would offer greater security within the organisation.

The truth of the matter was that he was a fugitive from justice. If caught, he would be condemned for murder.

Jim felt confused. He had joined the ILF because it seemed his duty to do so. How could he now be judged guilty? 'If you're not a spider, stay clear of the web!' Flaherty had warned. Now he was deeply entangled; and not just in a web of dangerous men, rather in a web of his own tortuous thoughts. The next three months should be some kind of retreat to sort himself out, Jim determined. He must return from India with a clear mind. He must resolve his conscience one way or the other.

FOURTEEN

Jim was too preoccupied with his own problems to pay much attention to the exuberant oriental streets of Bombay during their one day stop-over. While Paddy set off on a tourist spree, he walked around till he found a Catholic church, the Sacred Heart parish church in Villeparle, not far from their hotel.

He could not pray.

He sat down in the last pew and looked absentmindedly at the popular saints on their pedestals, flanking walls daubed with the blue and rose pastel tints so much favoured by Goans. He admired the simple people who came in every now and then to kneel before the sanctuary and say a fleeting prayer. At least they could pray.

How would these simple folk react if they knew he was a priest with blood on his hands? As likely as not they would run away from him in horror.

His gaze was drawn to a miniature battle scene on the floor next to the pew. A locust which had broken a wing was being attacked by a horde of large black ants. Some had already hooked their jaws onto its legs and wings. The locust wriggled and jumped to get free but the ants hung on and more and more of them dug their teeth into the insect's body. The struggle continued for at least ten minutes till the poor locust was held on all sides and stopped moving.

Jim was petrified at the sight. Was God telling him something? Reminding him of Peter Bowyer's struggle on that fateful night?

After Jim had tied Peter to the chair, Peter had regained consciousness sooner than Jim had let on about when talking to Bill. Peter had pleaded and argued.

92

'You call yourself a man of God? Kidnapping is an act of terrorism.'

'Shut up! You people are the real terrorists!'

'How original.'

'Not original. It's true. You object to being held but how many of our people have been held without charge or trial since internment began?'

'I demand that you release me immediately.'

'You've nothing to demand. This is our country.'

'I too am a citizen. I have a right to my freedom.'

'And what about the hunger strikers? Didn't they have the right to be accorded the political status they enjoyed before? What did the likes of you do? You crushed their protest, allowing ten to die and torturing the rest into submission.'

Jim knew he was being unfair. Peter Bowyer had been one of the prison governors who had pressed for a compromise.

'I'm a Christian', Peter started again. 'I believe we will stand one day before Christ's judgment seat. What will you as a priest tell him? Will he praise you for being a terrorist?'

'Nonsense. Your preaching won't help you. I know Christ is on my side.'

'Is he? How can he be on the side of crime? Tell me. I've always respected priests. Your bishops and your pope keep insisting Catholics should abandon violence and promote peace. Treat me at least as a fellow Christian and make me understand how you can justify violence.'

'Shut up!' Jim had said again.

But he had begun to talk all the same. He had wanted to fill the awkward vacuum of the wait. He had also felt a sudden need to explain himself to Peter. It was almost as if the roles had been reversed and it was his turn to plead, to ask for understanding.

'You talked about the last day. What will Christ say? He will say: 'Where were you when I was hungry, when I was sick, when I was in prison . . . . ? Whatever you did to the least of mine, you did to me . . . . '

'Don't you understand? As a priest I have to be with my

people. I have to be with them where they are: in their misery; in their being robbed of rights, jobs and houses; in their struggle for recognition and freedom. How can I say I'm truly Christ in their midst if I wash my hands of the violent situation forced upon them? That's why I know Christ will be on my side.'

'A Christ of your own making', Peter had scorned. 'The Christ I know from the Bible died on the cross rather than commit bloodshed .... What are you waiting for? Why don't you finish me off? Or are your priestly hands too sacred to kill but sacred enough to hand me over to one of your henchmen?'

It was then that Jim had realised for the first time that killing might indeed be Derry's response .... Sweat had broken out all over him at the thought. But what could he do? He had to wait for further instructions .... He had to trust the ILF to find a solution that would keep him out of murder ....

Soon after, Paddy had come. Peter had known instinctively from Paddy's attitude that he was to die. But Jim had been blind. He had wanted to believe Paddy's story about the amnesia-inducing drug.

That's when Peter had made his last plea to Jim.

'I still think you're a criminal and betraying Christ but at least you're a minister. Could you, please, do me a favour?'

'What favour?'

'I was married years ago and have a daughter called Evelyn. I've greatly wronged her in a way I've no time or wish to explain. Please, tell her I beg her forgiveness.'

'I will', Jim had said.

'Thank you. It makes me feel I can face my judgment with greater tranquillity, which is more than can be said for the pair of you .... Well, what are you waiting for?'

Then Paddy had taken a bottle from his pocket, sprinkled chloroform on a handkerchief and held it over Peter's face. Peter had slumped in the chair. Jim recalled with horror the events that followed; how they had dragged him upstairs into the bedroom, how they had pulled off Peter's suit and shirt and hung them in the wardrobe; how they had slipped on the pyjamas and laid him on the bed, under the blanket.

A few minutes later, while Jim was downstairs, Paddy had fired the shots that killed Peter.

As Bill had bluntly stated, he should have known. He knew the score. From Derry's point of view, there was no other option. It did not change the fact that he, Jim, was irrevocably mixed up with robbery, assault and murder. A killing remained a killing, even in war. He would have its stains on his conscience till the end of his life . . . .

Next day Jim and Paddy arrived at Hyderabad airport. They had been given no information about their hosts, apart from a recognition sign. The person to meet them would be eating grapes and asking for them by name, their new names, that is.

With the other passengers they walked across the tarmac to the arrival hall. Since this was an internal flight from Bombay, there was no need of passing through immigration or customs. The passengers were met in the arrival hall by throngs of friends and relatives. There were emotional scenes. A young man who had, perhaps, been abroad for studies was hugged and garlanded by a succession of brothers, sisters, uncles and aunts, cousins, nieces and nephews. 'What a welcome!' Jim thought.

They mingled in the crowd wondering what would happen. Suddenly a young Indian woman in a sari addressed them. She was strikingly beautiful. Her dark face was delicately carved. Her long black hair was tied in a knot at the back of her head and decorated with white flowers. Her eyes were dark brown - and direct. In her right hand she carried a bunch of grapes.

With a thin smile she stood before the two men.

'Are you Mr. Jim and Paddy Ferguson?'

'We are', Jim said. 'And who are you?'

'My name is Kameswari.' She pronounced it as 'Kah-mays-wah-ree'.

She put the grapes into her bag and shook hands.

'Welcome to Hyderabad.'

They collected their luggage. Kameswari chartered porters and walked ahead with them to where her car was parked.

'Wow', Paddy said to Jim. 'India may be more fun than I'd thought.'

FIFTEEN

Kameswari, it turned out, was a very interesting woman. Lecturer in history at Osmania University. Free-lance writer for half a dozen magazines. Collector of traditional Telugu weapons, and a keen archer in her free time. A woman inclined to take command and get things her own way. She was also a good hostess.

Jim and Paddy were each given a spacious room on the second floor of her magnificent house on Krishnamenon Avenue in the Banjara Hills area. Pouring them a glass of sherry in the lounge downstairs Kameswari spelled out the rules.

'You are two friends from England whom I got to know while studying in Oxford. You, Jim, have lost your wife. It affects you a lot so you've come to India to be away from home for a while. Patrick is your son who's come along to keep you company.'

'What a son!', Jim remarked. 'God help me.'

'I want both of you to be extremely cautious', Kameswari continued. 'Hyderabad has a fair number of foreigners but you should not stand out. For safety's sake I want you to move only within a small circle of friends to whom I will introduce you.'

'Understood', Jim said.

'Do you know why we are here?' Paddy asked.

'That's a silly question', Kameswari retorted. 'There are things I don't know and don't want to know. All I know is that you are friends. Let's keep it that way, shall we?'

'Sure', Paddy said.

That same evening Jim was introduced to Colonel Pattabhi Raghava Rao, stately, with an unmistakable military posture, middle-aged just like he was himself. Jim took to him.

'Call me 'Rao'', the Colonel said, 'so much easier'.

Rao had come over for supper. He proved a good conversationalist who possessed an inexhaustible treasure of tales from Indian army life. After supper Kameswari and Paddy talked in the lounge. Jim and Rao drifted out onto the balcony. They sat down in easy chairs, looking out over a small park across the road from Kameswari's house.

'I was in England years ago', Rao said, 'I'll never forget the experience.'

'Tell me', Jim urged.

'Well, it was pretty awful.'

'Tell me all the same.'

'It might hurt your national pride.'

'It won't', Jim said. 'I'm thick-skinned, I assure you. What happened?'

'Well, all right then. But don't say afterwards I didn't warn you. I was at the time, that's about ten years ago, in charge of an engineering company. It was our task to maintain the tanks of a tank division in Kashmir.

'Now I had under me a group of very intelligent lads. We Indians, believe me, can be extremely good engineers. We didn't invent motorcars perhaps, but we certainly know how to keep them running. You will have noticed how old many cars are over here .... Some lorries and trucks are forty or fifty years old. They've been in service all the time and are still running. Sometimes when you're on the road outside the big cities you'll find a lorry standing on the side; it may have broken down, but the driver will go underneath with his spanner and will get it going. Well, in my company I had some extremely gifted lads who knew the workings of the tank inside out.

'The tanks we were using at the time were Mayflower II, a British make. It was a good machine, but it had its shortcom-

98

ings. In particular, its gears were not strong enough. With sudden acceleration, the teeth of the crankshaft would get broken or twisted or dislodged, making the vehicle immobile and a sitting duck for enemy artillery.

'Well, my lads had worked out a solution that would permanently solve the problem. They had evolved a new design with a different kind of crankshaft and an intermediate gear. They made drawings and constructed a prototype. Because it was important for the army, we sent both to the British manufacturers. Receipt of our letter or the plans or the model was not even acknowledged.

'I was furious and decided to travel to England myself.

'When I arrived in Nottingham I had trouble in getting through to the Managing Director. When I did, I was in for an ugly surprise.

'He listened to what I had to say, then had the audacity to tell me: 'We never received your documents. But anyway, we ourselves have already introduced improvements such as you describe.'

'When I expressed my disbelief, he summoned a draughtsman who showed me the new plans. I could see at a glance that they were based on ours - with some small changes to mask the piracy.

'I was really furious but what proof did I have? Also, it wasn't in our interest to cause a rift with the firm on whom we depended for further supplies of tanks and spare parts. I really felt cheated, humiliated, defeated and hurt in my pride.'

'I don't blame you', Jim said. 'The Brits can rob and steal with an arrogance not matched by any other nation.'

'I thought you were English yourself', Rao observed slyly.

'I am, I am', Jim said. He could have kicked himself for his indiscretion. 'I'm only too aware of how often we take advantage of other people.'

'You may be a good soldier, you wouldn't get very far as a spy', Rao remarked again.

'I don't know what you're getting at', Jim said, now feeling very uncomfortable.

'Let's stop playing games', Rao stated. 'I know more than you're aware of. I was consulted about your coming to Hyderabad. You hate the English and so do I. That's one reason why we made you welcome.'

'And what's the other reason?'

'I'll tell you. There is a little job that needs doing over here and the two of you are just the right men to take it on.'

'What kind of job?'

'You'll hear about that later.'

'We're not here to do jobs - whatever it is you have in mind', Jim said firmly. 'We've not been told anything about it.'

'A serious omission', Rao replied. 'You will do the job because it was part of the deal. That's why we let you come.'

'We don't know anything about that and I'm not going to take your word for it.'

'You will', Rao said grimly.

Jim and Paddy walked to the Banjara shopping centre to buy a few odds and ends. Since Banjara is an upmarket area, the shops proved to be well-stocked and air-conditioned. They were all the more surprised, therefore, to see close by a rather primitive scene of washermen at work on what appeared to be a stretch of waste land.

On one side women were beating clothes on a concrete elevation surrounding a water tap. They would hold a wet garment with both hands, raise it high above their heads and strike it forcefully against the concrete. At some distance from them a couple of men were boiling clothes in an enormous tub which stood over a charcoal fire. Others, both men and women were spreading shirts, saris and lunghis on the sparse patches of grass to dry them in the sun.

'This is a trade electric washing machines are bound to wipe out', Jim observed.

They watched a washerman arrive with a new load of laundry. It was carried in two bulging bundles on the back of a donkey. The poor animal, thin and underfed, tottered under its burden. When it faltered, the washerman swore at it and struck it viciously with a cane on its left flank. The animal winced with pain. Jim and Paddy could see the raw flesh exposed by previous beatings.

'Damn!' Paddy said. 'See how the animal suffers!'

Without more ado he walked over to the man, tore the cane from his hand and broke it in two. The man began to yell in protest. The others, both men and women, stopped their work and came to the man's rescue. Passers-by from the road came running up as well so that Paddy, Jim, the donkey and the donkey's driver were soon surrounded by an agitated crowd.

A gentleman with a briefcase under his arm - must be a clerk, Jim thought - offered to mediate.

'What's the trouble?'

'This effin' fellow is hurting the animal', Paddy said.

His face was flushed with anger as he indicated the torn flesh on the donkey's flank. Some stripes showed fresh blood. Others oozed pus that attracted dark green flies. Jim could see tears in Paddy's eyes as he examined the wounds. He stroked the donkey as if to assure it that its suffering would soon be over.

'Correct, sir. This man is cruel', the gentleman said.

He turned to the washer people and harangued them in Telugu with a genuine edge of indignation to his voice.

An elderly man spoke in return. The gentleman translated.

'He says the donkey is lazy, doesn't want to work.'

Another avalanche of words from the senior washerman.

'He says the treatment of a donkey is up to the owner. If you like the animal, why don't you buy it?'

'For how much?' Paddy asked.

'Ten thousand rupees.'

'That's far too much', the translator added. 'Let me bargain for you.'

The two men began to haggle in Telugu to the amusement

of the crowd.

'Four thousand rupees is the lowest he will go', the translator reported.

'Done!' Paddy said. 'That's only 160 pounds', he added for Jim's benefit.

'What on earth are you going to do with a flipping donkey?' Jim retorted.

'Shut your face', Paddy said.

He pulled out his wallet and paid the money. The driver took the bundles of clothes from the donkey's back, tied a lead round the donkey's neck and handed the end of the lead to Paddy.

'Take it', the mediator said. 'By holding the lead you become the owner.'

People stared after Jim and Paddy as they walked back with the donkey.

'My grand dad was a milkman', Paddy said suddenly. 'He used a horse and cart to deliver the milk. The horse was a grey. Its name was Pearl; I loved it. I washed it and played a lot with it when I was a kid. Donkeys are as sensitive as horses I reckon.'

'Right', Jim said.

Kameswari was amused when the men returned with the donkey.

'Let's give it to my gardener', she suggested. 'I'll make sure he looks after it well.'

'I forgot to ask its name', Paddy said.

'Its name? Donkeys have no names in our country.'

'I'll call it Hardy', Paddy announced.

He insisted on washing the animal, brushing it down, tending to its wounds and feeding it before handing it over to the gardener.

SIXTEEN

A few days later Kameswari took Jim and Paddy on a sight-seeing tour of old Hyderabad. They spent most of the morning in Salar Jung Museum, the permanent record of a Nawab's insatiable curiosity. The nineteenth century prince had collected everything under the sun: precious jewel-studded swords and hand- printed Deccan miniatures as well as European furniture, coffee grinders, tea trays, doormats and bedpans. Jim was not really impressed. Paddy kept asking questions but more to engage Kameswari's attention, Jim felt sure, than out of real interest.

They walked to the Charminar through small shopping streets. Old Hyderabad is inhabited by Urdu- speaking Muslims who have preserved from the Arab and Persian ancestors that labyrinth of shop-lined lanes and alleys known as the *suq*. It reminded Jim of Jerusalem where he had seen, heard and smelled the identical reality. The streets were almost like tunnels. Shops on either side displayed their oriental wares - whether embroidered shalwar-kamises, brass pots, coloured cakes, music cassettes or fruit, so prominently that the milling crowds were forced to brush against the merchandise.

They reached the Charminar, a tall rectangular three-story gate flanked by four elegant towers. They entered one of them. When they had climbed up to the top by a narrow, spiralling stairway inside the tower, they were rewarded with a panoramic view. Flat-roofed stone buildings of all sizes could be seen in all directions, an ocean of human artifacts fringed by the occasional green of trees and palms. Some buildings could be picked out easily, the tribunal, Osmania Hospital, the Falaknuma Palace, the Mecca Mashid Mosque with its high walls and tall minarets. But in between lay the grey mass of indistinguishable houses.

'This is a favourite spot for people to commit suicide', Kameswari remarked.

Jim looked down at the square below and shuddered.

'Why here?', Paddy asked.

'Originally, because it was founded as a place of sorrow', Kameswari said. 'People came here to weep and mourn. Now it's become something of a tradition.'

When Kameswari and Paddy made ready to go down, Jim sat down on a ledge and waved at them.

'You go on', he said. 'I prefer to stay here. I'll come back by taxi later.'

'I hope you're not thinking of jumping down', Paddy teased.

Jim did not even bother to reply.

'I was going to take you to a restaurant for lunch', Kameswari said.

'Never mind', Jim said. 'I don't feel like eating anyway. I'll survive.'

Two minutes later he was on his own.

The view over the oriental city reminded Jim once more of Jerusalem. He had been sitting on the roof of the Coptic convent. Surveying the mass of buildings, he had cursed the Holy City because his mind had been in turmoil. He recalled the agony of those days and the hard decisions he had had to make. Once he had made up his mind, everything else had followed on naturally. It was because of his commitment at the time that he had become what he was: a militant crusader.

Jim had always been in sympathy with the Republican cause. Having grown up in the Falls Road area he carried in his guts the sense of the enormous injustice inflicted on his people. In the seminary he had repeatedly argued the case for the IRA. He had been reprimanded more than once by his superiors for what had been called 'foolish indiscretion and uncontrolled temper'. As a young priest he had a number of times alluded to the freedom struggle in his sermons. He had been admonished about this by his parish priest, even the bishop. But never had he considered taking up arms himself. He had felt it to be inappropriate to his role as a priest - till his father got killed. That changed everything.

Jim recalled the heated discussions he had had with his father, a respected member of the Irish Liberation Front.

'Look at my hand', his father had said, clenching a huge workman's fist. 'God has given us bones and nails and the power to strike. Unless we use that power, no one will take note.'

'Who lifts the sword, will die by the sword', Jim had told him.

'Rubbish. Whether we like it or not, the world is ruled by the laws of the jungle. The strongest survives. If you meet a rat, you kill it. That's how God has made the world.'

'But what's the use of killing innocent people?'

'In this game there are no innocent people. A pig is a pig, whether it's a female pig or a baby pig. A scorpion remains a scorpion whatever its sex. The Brits are the enemy. We have to fight them till we gain our independence. There's no place for softness.'

'That's hardly a Christian view. Does the Gospel not demand love and mercy, even towards one's enemies?'

'Rubbish! It doesn't apply when survival is at stake.'

'It always applies.'

'No, it doesn't. And don't preach at me. Why have a handful of Brits managed to conquer Ireland? Why can they keep us as slaves in our own country? Because priests like you have made them soft. There is a time when mercy and love should be preached, perhaps; but there are also times when priests should encourage the people to stand up, to fight, to shed their blood if necessary.'

'To preach war?'

'Yes. The Bible is full of it. God is no softy. He is as hard and tough as the rock of Lough Derg. He expected his son to die on a cross!'

Jim remembered Rosaleen's death, the vigil he had spent in Bishop Street church, in front of the crucifix. He knew his father had a point. God was hard, in a mysterious kind of way. He had wanted his son, Jesus, to die, as he had wanted Rosaleen to die. All this talk of God's love . . . .

Shortly afterwards his father had been killed, shot by loyalists in Prince Road pub. Two masked men carrying automatic pistols had entered, looked for their quarry and riddled his body with bullets. Those who witnessed the scene said he had not uttered a word. He had died with the dignity of an old Celtic warrior.

The event had deeply shaken Jim. In one stroke he had lost a mentor whom he admired and a father whom he loved. He had been numb with sorrow and anger. Unable to control his emotions in public, he had declined, at the last moment, to conduct the funeral Mass himself. But sadness had gradually made way for another feeling. As his father's body was escorted to the grave by hundreds of supporters, almost carried in triumph and given military honours, he had felt elated and proud. His father had been a hero, a martyr for the cause he believed in. Compared to him Jim had suddenly felt worthless and small.

The pilgrimage to the Holy Land two months later had come at the right time. There were some other priests in the group so he could often excuse himself and be on his own. He wanted to sort things out, to think his position through.

One aspect of Israel had struck him immediately. It was a hard country. In particular the province of Judea around Jerusalem was a land of barren soil and rock. In some places it was classical desert, hill after hill without water or a blade of grass. Calling this a land of milk and honey was an atrocious euphemism. Why had God settled his chosen people in such a tough country? Could his father have been right by saying God is as hard as rock?

The country is also a country of bloodshed. Not a square mile can be found on the map that is not marked by conflict or battle, whether in ancient or in modern times. Even more surprising was the fact that a good deal of the bloodshed had been ordered by God himself.

On the top of Mount Pisgah, east of Jericho, from which Moses had looked across the Jordan into the Holy Land Jim reflected on this mystery. He had a copy of the Bible with him and he decided to read the relevant passages with an open mind. Deuteronomy stated it clearly in chapter twenty.

'When you go out to fight against your enemies, do not be impressed by their chariots and horses or by their superior numbers . . . . Yahweh, your God, is going into battle ahead of you. He will give you the victory . . . . And when you conquer cities in this land that Yahweh your God is giving you, kill everyone. Completely destroy all the people: the Hittites, the Amorites, the Canaanites, the Perizzites, the Hivites and the Jebusites. Yahweh himself orders you to do so. Kill all of them.'

Before Joshua entered Jericho, he issued this command: *'Yahweh has given the city into our hands. The town and all people in it must be totally destroyed as an offering to Yahweh.'* And that is what happened. *'With their swords the Israelites put to death everyone in the city, men and women, young and old. Even the cattle were killed, and the sheep and donkeys.'*

The same treatment was meted out to the neighbouring town, Ai. *'Joshua kept his spear pointed at Ai until every person in it had been put to death. The whole population of Ai was killed that day - twelve thousand men and women.'*

Jim put his Bible down. There was no doubt about it. At God's explicit command whole nations had been massacred. Why? To make way for the chosen people to whom it had been promised. What about the previous inhabitants? How could God simply dispense with them? There was a hardness there that Jim feared and at the same time admired. Perhaps, his father had been right. Perhaps, he was discovering the true nature of God, infinitely more frightening than the sweet Jesus held out to him by the nuns at school.

But did it make sense from a Christian point of view? Had the hardness of the Old Testament not been abolished by the love and mercy of the New?

Insight about this had dawned on him some days later as he was surveying Jerusalem from the roof of the Coptic convent. He had been staring at the black dome that covers Calvary, the rock on which Jesus had died.

As his father had told him, if the New Testament God had lost his hardness, why had he wanted his son to die? Jesus Christ had begged him: 'Let this chalice pass me by.' The Father had not listened. He had wanted his son to die a gruesome death on a cross firmly implanted into the rock.

There had been other moments and other reasons but that day in Jerusalem had helped him to make up his mind. After his return to Northern Ireland, he had sought contact with the ILF. They had been extremely cautious. He had been given small assignments till they trusted him. Although he received the rank of lieutenant, Derry and his high command had kept his membership secret from other members. 'You're a priest. You'll be very useful to us - one day', he had been told. He had been lying low for years, till he had been called to active service two weeks ago.

What a traumatic event it had been. He shivered and felt hungry.

He descended the narrow steps leading down and looked for a place to eat.

SEVENTEEN

Kameswari and Paddy were becoming close friends; so close, in fact, that Jim began to worry about them. He would never have thought that such an unlikely pair could get entangled. She was after all ten years older, more educated, even more intelligent he would have thought. She was typically Hindu and culturally eastern. But they never seemed to tire of each other's company.

Jim took a seat on the balcony of the lounge when he noticed the two sitting on the grass of the little park across the road. She was talking. Paddy hung at her lips, his boyish admiration apparent even at such a distance.

Kameswari owned a pair of binoculars, Jim knew. He went inside the lounge and took it from the glass cupboard in which it stood displayed. Resuming his seat on the balcony without having been observed, he focused the binoculars on the two.

She was sitting on the grass with her legs stretched in front. He was lying next to her on his right elbow. Both had put off their shoes. Jim could clearly see that while they were talking, they were touching each other with their bare feet. It was a small thing in itself but it came as a shock to Jim. It confirmed the fact that a new stage of intimacy had been reached.

That afternoon, when Kameswari had gone out to do some shopping, Jim tackled Paddy on the question.

'You've taking a fancy to Miss K, haven't you?'

'So what?'

'Well, it could go too far, you know.'

'It's none of your business.'

'It is my business. For one thing it's a security risk.'

'It's not. Are you jealous?'

109

'Certainly not.'

'Then why don't you leave me alone? I can look after myself.'

'So can you? And what if you make her pregnant? Are you prepared to marry her?'

'Who knows?' Paddy said. 'If I want to, what's there to stop me?'

'I am. Because I know it wouldn't work out. It would not be fair on the girl. It would create complications you might not be able to handle. Think of your parents and the rest of your family at home.'

Paddy's face grew red with anger.

'Keep my family out of this. Who are you anyway? For all I know, you're just bloody jealous of me. Let me tell you straight. If you ever talk about this again, I'll beat you to pulp. I won't be able to hold back.'

'Calm down, man', Jim said. 'You're young. I've seen people get into trouble by just a few hours of stupidity. I'm trying to talk sense into you before you're head-over-heels in love with her. Don't forget, I'm your commander on this operation. I'm responsible for you.'

'Shit!' Paddy said.

He turned away and went to his own room.

Next day Rao came and talked with Kameswari for a long time. Eventually they convoked what turned out to be a consultation.

'For reasons we cannot disclose to you, we will have to move the two of you to a village a hundred and fifty miles north of here', Rao disclosed.

'That's a pity', Paddy said. 'I was just getting used to this place.'

'I'm afraid there's no other option', Kameswari replied smiling at him. 'I'll remain in touch with you. The place you'll be going to is my home village.'

'Oh, that's great', Paddy said.

'Can't you tell us a little more?' Jim prodded. 'We seem perfectly safe here.'

'Safety is one consideration', Rao said, carefully choosing his words. 'You are much safer in the village because you're out of the reach of any foreigner or even the State police. But it also brings you closer to your target.'

'Our target?'

'Yes.'

'I don't follow you.'

'I talked to you about the job you'll have to do. Staying in the village is a preparation. It will make you familiar with the overall scene.'

'I haven't the least intention of being involved in the job you're talking about,' Jim replied with some vehemence.

'What job?' Paddy asked.

'Haven't a clue', Jim said. 'They're going to use us for some private purpose.'

'Don't be so hostile', Kameswari intervened. 'We are your friends, aren't we? And we haven't been able to explain the circumstances to you. Can't you give us your confidence? Aren't you willing to help us in return for all the hospitality we are giving you?' She opened her eyes widely, looking at Paddy.

'Of course we will', Paddy answered. He almost drooled with eagerness to please her.

'I'm the one to decide that', Jim said firmly. 'I'm not making any promises until we know what it is you want.'

'Fair enough! Well spoken!' Rao said with an air of condescension that angered Jim. 'You don't need to decide now. We'll explain everything to you at the proper time. I trust you will not let us down when the challenge is put to you. Meanwhile, we will move you to your new residence.'

To facilitate the journey Rao lent his own Landrover and his driver. Kameswari was coming along. She brought air guns so that they could do some hunting in a forest they would pass on the way. 'Why not make the most of life?' she had said.

During the journey Jim was sitting next to the driver. Kameswari and Paddy were sitting at the back. As usual, the woman was chatting away while Paddy kept her going with occasional questions. He wondered if more was going on but he did not dare to turn his head and look.

They arrived at Yerrapandimoola, the place for the hunt. The Landrover turned into a dust track that ran through shrubs and undergrowth for a couple of miles, then halted at a small clearing. A cloth was spread on the stubby, low grass. Tiffin carriers with tins of steaming rice and a variety of curries were placed on its side. It was the beginning of a delicious lunch, surprisingly luxurious in such a wild and deserted place.

When the meal was over, Kameswari distributed the guns.

'This jungle is full of wild fowl', she said. 'There are also deer, a spotted variety we call *jinka* and, if we're lucky, we may come across a small kind of tiger, the *chinnapuli*. Most of these animals will be resting in the shade because of the noon heat. Our best strategy is to walk through the undergrowth keeping our guns in readiness.'

They walked abreast, at about twenty yards' distance from each other. Occasionally one of them would shoot. Kameswari and Paddy had bagged a few fowl each which they gave to the driver to carry. Jim did not have his heart in the business. He saw a few birds but saw no point in shooting them.

Suddenly Kameswari stood beside him. They were standing on top of a hillock in the shadow of an old banyan tree. It rose majestically over their heads. Below them lay a grove of *thumma* trees, the thorny, sinewy shrubs that can survive even the driest summer. At the far side, on top of one of the trees, they could see a white heron. It was a hundred yards away.

'It's yours', Kameswari whispered and taunted him with her smile.

Jim was too much a sportsman not to rise to the challenge. His secret training with the ILF was now going to pay off.

He raised his gun, aimed carefully and pulled the trigger.

112

The heron jumped up, fluttered and fell down.

'Good!' Kameswari cried.

She ran ahead to look for the bird. Jim suddenly realised what she had done: she had tested his skill as a marksman. He resented it. He had not really needed to kill the heron.

Dusk had already fallen when they arrived at their destination, Yuddhapalli. The Landrover drove through dusty streets with plenty of potholes. The mud-wall houses looked grey and dull. 'This is really the end of the world', Jim thought.

They stopped at a low archway. It led into a large compound, sparsely lit by weak electric lights along the inside walls. Jim saw at a glance the three buffaloes tethered near a rubbish dump at the far side, a well on the other side, and in the middle towards the back two bungalows, one larger, the other one smaller.

Kameswari led them to the verandah of the larger bungalow. An old lady came out, dressed in a white sari, leaning on a stick. Three servants, two boys and a girl, came running from the kitchen. The old lady gave a sign to the girl. She handed Kameswari a round tray with flower wreaths coiled on top of it.

Kameswari took one, stood in front of Jim, hung the wreath round his neck and said 'Welcome to Yuddhapalli'. She repeated the same rite for Paddy. Then she greeted the old lady with a hug and told Jim and Paddy. 'This is my mother. You will be guests in my ancestors' house, the Yeddanapudi home. My mother is happy to receive you.'

'What about your father?' Jim asked.

'He is no longer alive. My three sisters have all married so my mother lives alone in the house.'

Jim and Paddy stepped forward. The old lady did not offer to shake hands. She folded her hands in the *vandana* gesture and bowed in greeting without saying a word. Jim looked at her wrinkled face and saw two strong, penetrating eyes that seemed to size him up with the perception of some unspeakable wisdom.

While supper was being prepared for them on the verandah of the main bungalow, Jim and Paddy were conducted to the smaller one that served as the guest quarters. For some time two of her sisters had lived here, Kameswari explained.

Each received a separate room, with a bathroom that contained a low-level, Indian toilet.

When Jim's luggage had been put in his room, he decided to have a bath first. He felt sweaty and dirty.

He locked the room with a bolt provided on the inside of the door. He undressed, leaving his clothes in a pile on the bed. Naked he walked into the bathroom. In a large empty bucket he mixed water from a tub with cold water and a bronze pot with hot water, as Kameswari had shown them. When the water was of the right temperature, he scooped it up with a small pan- like *chembu* that had been provided. It was delicious to feel the water splash on his head and shoulders and down his body.

In the middle of these ablutions, he heard a noise in his room. Without further ado he dropped the *chembu* into the bucket and entered the room, still naked. He was just in time to see a young man climb out of the window. Jim ran after him. At the window he saw the man run across the compound and out of the archway into the dark street beyond.

Jim cursed. He closed the window and examined it. He had forgotten to bolt it! Looking back into the room he saw that his case had been broken open and searched. Even the clothes he had been wearing were lying on the floor.

Whoever the intruder had been, he had left his passport and his money. But the revolver had gone. It frightened and puzzled Jim. Could the thief have known he possessed the weapon and that he was to stay in that room? It seemed highly unlikely. But if he had been a casual thief, why pick this moment and restrict himself to that object?

The loss of the weapon and the mystery surrounding the theft made Jim feel as insecure as ever. He decided he would not tell Paddy or Kameswari.

EIGHTEEN

Yuddhapalli was bigger than Jim had thought. The village prided itself on having 5000 inhabitants, Kameswari told them. These people belonged to sixteen different castes. The ruling caste were the Reddies who, though small in number, were rich farmers. They owned most of the land. Their rivals, the Kammas, were also farmers but their economic strength had declined in recent years. There were a number of intermediate castes, each with their own quarter in the village: the weavers, the potmakers, the shepherds, the merchants, the toddy-tappers, the washermen and the woodworkers. At the bottom of the social ladder but most numerous were the Malas and Madigas who lived in small huts on the periphery of the village and who worked as coolies and land labourers for daily wages.

As Jim discovered when they were taken through the village by Kameswari, the village was a miniature world, almost self-supporting and self-contained.

They arrived at an old banyan tree in the middle of the village. Its wide canopy of leaves provided shade for an open square as large as a tennis court. Its stem was surrounded by a raised platform of solid stone - the traditional meeting place for the village elders, Kameswari told them. Close to the tree stood, six feet high on a marble pedestal, the statue of a young man. A wreath of fresh flowers had been placed on his shoulders.

'This is a memorial to Prataparudra Deva, the son of the village Brahmin', Kameswari explained. 'He was a disciple of Potti Sriramulu who fasted to death in 1952 to demand that an autonomous State be created for the Telugus. Like his master Prataparudra died for the cause. The villagers are proud of him. His old father, who is still alive, decorates the statue with fresh flowers every single day.'

'Each village is governed by an elected council', Kameswari continued. 'We call it the *panchayat*, a Sanscrit word that means 'council of five'. I'm going to introduce you to the panchayati president. I don't like the man. He is a bully. He exploits the poor. He got himself elected by bribing the Malas and Madigas with five rupees a head on the day before the elections. Not introducing you to him would be a tactical error.'

Standing on the verandah of the great man's house, Jim could see he must be rich. Five spans of bullocks were just being led out of the compound, dragging ploughs on wheels after them.

'Meet Madhura Yella Reddy', Kameswari said pointing at a huge and heavy individual who was reclining in an armchair on the verandah. His white khurta and wide pyjama trousers bulged on all sides, making the man look like an elephant lying on his back. Two slits in his puffed up face hinted at the place where his eyes must be.

Without making an effort to raise himself, he lifted his fleshy arm and shook hands.

'Welcome. Welcome. And why have you come?'

'I met Mr. Ferguson and his son while studying in Oxford', Kameswari said.

'Aha. But why have they come?'

'They're my friends.'

'Of course. Can't they speak for themselves?'

Kameswari blushed with annoyance. Jim helped her by speaking up.

'My wife died. I was very much attached to her. I thought it would do me good to be away from home for a while so I took a long holiday and am travelling round the world to see some of my friends, like Kameswari.'

'How long will you be staying in the village?'

'I don't know yet. I will see.'

'You have not prepared a schedule for the rest of your

116

journey?'

Madhura looked dubiously at him through the narrow slits of his eyes.

'Vaguely. It's very flexible.'

'Our village has little entertainment. No television, no cinema, no theatre. We have no tourist facilities.'

One moment Jim hesitated. The man was no fool. Only bluff would do.

'We have not come as tourists. We are sick of city life with all its complications. We want to enjoy the Indian countryside, to share the simple life-style of the people here. We want to taste the peace and tranquillity we did not find in our own country.'

'I hope you'll find it here', Madhura said with a thinly veiled note of sarcasm.

Then he dismissed them.

'If I can be of assistance to you, please let me know.'

'The Yeddanapudi home will give them all they need', Kameswari said testily.

'Of course, of course. Since they're your friends . . . . '

Once outside the compound, Kameswari burst out in anger.

'The swine! I hate that man. You handled him well Jim, I must say. But you can see that he's a dangerous opponent.'

The word 'opponent' rang in Jim's ears as Kameswari showed them the other sights of the village: a shopping street with seven shops; the forty-feet deep well used by caste women to draw drinking water; a temple to Nageshwara, the lion-headed god; a pentecostal church in the Mala quarter and a Catholic church among the Madiga huts; a dispensary and a girls school run by a convent of nuns.

'Are you a Kamma?' Jim asked.

'Yes', Kameswari answered. 'I'm a Pedda Kamma and I wouldn't want to be anything else.'

Two days later was a Sunday. Jim had found out that a priest would come from outside to say Mass at ten o'clock. At half past nine he entered the simple church building. It was almost completely bare inside: rough brick walls, a tin roof, holes that could be boarded up, for windows. There were no pews or benches, only reed mats spread on the mud floor. On the far side a table served as the altar. An Indian Sister, who was wearing a light blue sari as her religious uniform, had begun to decorate it with a white altar cloth and a pair of candles.

Some men, obviously coolies judging by their workworn hands and tattered clothes, were already sitting on the floor. Jim joined them. He found it difficult to sit cross-legged but he managed quite well on the floor once he propped up his legs and sat with his back against the wall.

A motorbike could be heard outside. It stopped. A few moments later a young Indian priest came in. He spoke briefly to the Sister, then began to hear confessions, sitting on a chair near the altar. More and more people entered and sat down, men on the right, women with and without babies on the left. The space round the altar was kept free. Jim wondered why. He understood when he saw some other Sisters, wearing the same uniform, marching boys and girls of school going age. They sat down round the altar.

The school children began to sing Telugu songs. The older people chimed in, as well as they could. The singing was not particularly beautiful. Quite a few voices were harsh and out of tune. Yet Jim felt strangely touched. After all these days in a strange land he now felt at home. These were simple folk, the poor, people whose lives were hard as the lives of the dock workers and labourers he had known in Belfast. These people were believing Christians as his folk at home who clung to their faith in God for lack of anything better in the world.

Jim began to cry. He did not know why but a flood of tears flowed from his eyes and could not be stopped. The priest began Mass. A Sister read from the lectionary. Then the priest himself read and preached a sermon. Though the language spoken was Telugu, Jim knew what was being said. He looked on through the film of tears on his eyes and tried to fathom the depth of emotion that had been unleashed in him.

A medley of images had welled up. He tasted again the poverty at home, the resentment of carrying an inferior social stigma. He heard the crash of the explosion. He felt the warm blood sticking to his hands. He relived the conflicts with his father, his inner struggles about joining the ILF. He even saw the face of his mother as he remembered her from his pre-seminary days. There was no logic in these images, just pain; and a sense of despair.

The priest continued Mass. Jim knelt on both knees during consecration, as the others did. He exchanged greetings as well as he could with those sitting around him during the giving of peace. But when communion began, he was paralysed.

He felt a strong urge to walk up to the front and receive communion. It was a hunger for recognition, to be accepted again as a priest of God, to seal his unity with this community, to feel at peace with God. But his inner unease withheld him. He had blood on his hands. Though he had wanted to do his duty, he knew there was guilt too, a stain on his conscience that needed to be expiated.

When Mass was finished, people left the church in a hurry. Since most of them were coolies, they would need to work even on Sundays, Jim guessed. The priest laid off his vestments, walked through the area where the nuns and the schoolchildren were completing their thanksgiving and came up to Jim. Jim rose and they shook hands.

'Who are you?'

'Jim Ferguson from England.'

'Why have you come here?'

'I'm staying with a friend I got to know when she was studying in Oxford.'

'Oh, how nice! Are you a Catholic?'

'Yes, I am.'

'Why didn't you go to communion? You are most

welcome.'

Jim bit his tongue. What a question to ask. The young man still needed a lot of pastoral experience.

'Well, I haven't been going to church for some time . . . .   ', Jim said, with a blank expression on his face.

'Oh. Like that. If ever you want to go to confession, you can do so before Mass. I come especially early for that.'

'Thank you, Father.'

They shook hands again. The priest went to fetch his crash helmet, left the church and started the motorbike. 'No doubt on the way to another outstation' Jim thought.

At a sign of one of the sisters, the schoolchildren began to march out. The sisters too turned round and it was then that Jim discovered one of them was an Anglo-Indian.

She was a middle-aged person with a strikingly beautiful face of light brown complexion. She looked at Jim with large hazel eyes and a wide smile as she introduced herself.

'I'm Sister Sundari Frances. I'm principal of the girls' high school.

'Jim Ferguson from England.'

She smiled again. 'You may be living in England but you're not from England. What part of Ireland are you from?'

Jim swallowed. She'd recognised his accent!

'I'm from Belfast.'

'I studied in Dublin. I overheard Father talking to you. Don't mind him. He's got a lot to learn.'

Jim blushed.

'I'm happy to meet someone from Ireland', Sundari continued. 'I really got a liking for the place when I was there. Why don't you have tea with me this afternoon, at the convent?'

'To go to confession to you?' Jim said.

'Yes. Why not?'

Both laughed.

'What about Paddy . . . . , my son?' Jim said.

'He's welcome too. Bring him along.'

'Why didn't you tell us one of the nuns in the convent studied in Ireland?' Jim asked Kameswari at lunch.

'Oh, you mean Sister Sundari? I'd forgotten. She's been ten years in our village and speaks Telugu like one of us.'

'Studied in Ireland?' Paddy said.

'Yes. She's invited us to tea this afternoon. Are you coming along?'

'No. Kames is leaving us tomorrow for some days. We've arranged to go out for a walk.'

He winked at her.

NINETEEN

At four o'clock Jim presented himself at the convent. Sundari introduced him to the other three Sisters: Venanzia, Fidelis and Carmel Mary. Tea was served in the parlour. Biscuits and sweets of various kinds had been prepared for a do in which all took part.

The Sisters were highly amused hearing Jim's first impressions of India. He told them of his fight with half a dozen mosquitoes during his first night in Bombay. They rolled with laughter as he described how he had not been able to sleep because every time another mosquito would come roaring in, circling overhead, then suddenly dive-bomb onto his face.

Half an hour later Sundari suggested she should show Jim the various activities of the small mission centre. Jim agreed. He visited the dispensary, heard of the Sisters' difficulty in obtaining medicine and finding a doctor willing to come on regular visits. He saw the school buildings, capable of holding a thousand children in both the primary and high school levels. Ninety per cent of the children were non-Christian, he learned. The Christian children came mainly from backward castes and needed special protection.

Sundari's real pride was the girls' boarding school.

'We look after a hundred children from other villages. These are all Christian. They would not have a chance of attending school if we did not keep them here. Their parents are mostly very poor so that from donations of benefactors we ourselves have to pay for their food and their clothing.'

The boarding school consisted of three square rooms, built of concrete. The girls were divided over these rooms according

122

to their age groups. The rooms served as dormitories at night, dining rooms during the day and study halls in the evening. For hygiene there were toilets and washrooms outside. Each girl possessed a mat to sleep on, which could be rolled up and laid aside during the day, and an iron box to keep her clothes and other belongings in. Since it was a Sunday afternoon, the girls were playing outside. They all came running up, surrounded Sundari and Jim and plied them with a thousand questions in Telugu.

Sundari answered their questions and said to Jim: 'I'm telling them that you are from a country that I know, that you have come to India because you find it such a beautiful country and that you are staying with friends in the village.'

'Tell them that I am very happy to get to know them', Jim said.

The children clapped their hands when Sundari translated the greeting.

'You are from Belfast?', Sundari said as they continued their walk outside the village. 'It must be a hard place to live in.'

'It sure is', Jim said.

'A friend of mine sends me magazines from Ireland sometimes. It's awful to read of all the terrorist attacks. I can't understand how even Catholics take part in them.'

'The Catholic community has suffered a lot.'

'I know.'

'The IRA and like-minded organisations believe Catholics too have a right to defend themselves.'

'Of course.'

'Unless Catholics stand up and be counted they will remain oppressed for ever.'

'But does that justify murder?'

'What do you mean with murder?'

'What else to call the shooting down of people in their homes or the explosion of bombs in public places?'

'There is a reason for that'.

Sundari stopped walking and turned to look Jim in the face.

'Do you really believe you can justify killing people like that?'

A flush of anger came to Jim's face.

'Of course I do. I don't justify killing, but I do justify war.'

'Tell me', Sundari said, continuing her walk.

'The Catholics of Northern Ireland are slaves in their own country. The country in reality belongs to them. They will never be liberated until they are given back their full independence, whether this means union with the South or founding a new state. But such an independence will never be gained without war.'

'But that's a delusion!'

'It's not! We are engaged in a real war of liberation. A foreign enemy has occupied our country. Its troops outnumber ours. Its supplies of arms dwarf anything we can muster. What else can we do but use every means to unsettle the enemy? Our guerrilla attacks on political leaders and army personnel have been highly successful.'

'And what about innocent people? Bombs that kill and maim even women and children?'

'They are terrible, I know. They should be avoided. On the other hand, we need to acknowledge that they too serve a purpose. They strike fear in the general public. They make the Brits put pressure on their political leaders to end the occupation of Ireland.'

'And you really believe that kind of practice can be justified by Catholics?'

'At times, yes. During the Second World War the allies bombed German cities. Hundreds of thousands of civilians were killed. Did Catholics not take part in that? Politicians, generals, wing commanders and pilots? What is different between that and exploding a bomb in a supermarket frequented by enemy civilians?'

124

'You frighten me', Sundari said. 'You speak as if you are personally involved'.

'Of course I'm personally involved. We all are. In a struggle of this nature there can be no innocent bystanders. One either defends one's country or one is a traitor.'

In silence the two walked on along a path that wound between tobacco fields and ended up on the side of a small river.

'Let's sit here for a while', Sundari said.

'My father belonged to a Nationalist organisation', Jim said. His voice had lost its sharpness. It was soft and bitter.

'I adored my father. He was a strict man, even authoritarian at times. I was afraid of him when I was small; as were my six brothers and sisters. When he was angry, the whole house would tremble and shake. But he also had a good heart. He took a personal interest in each one of us. And all his life he worked hard as a dock worker to keep us alive and to earn our school fees.

'One day when I'd come home late, he gave me a whack that sent me sprawling on the floor. 'To bed with you, without food!' he shouted. I crawled out of his presence and went upstairs. I cried as I lay under the blankets. I could not sleep that whole night, not because he had beaten me or given me nothing to eat, but because he had not kissed me 'good night'. I was so happy when he hugged me next morning saying 'Never again son. Don't rouse my temper again.'

'Do you know what happened to him? Seven years ago he was shot down by Loyalists while he was drinking a beer in a pub. Neither the police nor the army interfered. His murderers got away. He was killed in the country that was his by rights. How could I not be involved in the freedom struggle of my people?'

'I'm sorry', Sundari said.

'How did you come to study in Ireland?', Jim asked.

'That's quite a story', Sundari replied.

'I'd like to hear it.'

Sundari hesitated.

'All right', she said. 'But some of it is very personal. Please, don't tell your son.'

'I won't', Jim promised.

'You see, I was born in India, in Poona. When my father got a job in Ireland, he took my mother and me with him. I was only six at the time. Then I lost my father, but my mother and I stayed on in Dublin.'

'I'm sorry you lost your father', Jim said. 'But why did the two of you not return to India?'

'It's very complicated. One day I may explain it all to you. One factor certainly was that single women are not treated well in India so my mother would be better off in Dublin. Also I had just begun going to school and my mother was anxious to give me the best possible education.

'We were very poor, I tell you. We had to live on a pitiable pension. I don't know how my mother managed. We lived in a small flat, three stories high. We could only afford the absolute basics in food and dress. In winter we could stay warm only by living in the kitchen. Sometimes when I returned from school, I would find my mother sitting in her armchair wrapped in our two blankets and still shivering with cold. Small wonder that she died young, during my last year at college.'

Sundari paused. Jim did not interrupt her. The memories of her childhood were flooding back and they overwhelmed her.

'My mother was a convinced Hindu and she remained like that all her life. She insisted that I too retain the Hindu way of life. She didn't realise that her stand put an enormous pressure on me. Inside our home we would perform *pooja* before our family shrine and read from the *Bhagavadgita*. In school I had to take part in the prayers, religious functions and catechism classes that were part of the daily schedule. Everybody knew I was a Hindu and still I had to take part.

'I felt it most in High School. I hated the nuns and I hated everything Catholic. You mustn't forget, I had all the odds against me. My clothes were always the same and old. I had a dark skin. I couldn't afford a complete set of class books. I had to borrow some to do my homework. On top of all that I was called 'the pagan'. Children can be cruel to each other. Often I had to fight for myself. On one occasion when a group of boys kept calling 'pagan! pagan' after me, I chased them till I'd got one of them pinned to the ground under my knees. I would have scratched out his eyes, if they'd let me.

'The girls were cruel too, in more subtle ways. One of them I considered my arch-enemy. She was called Monica. She looked like a doll, with long fair hair that would fall down to her shoulders. Boys always flocked around her. Her parents were well off, so she always had the best. She had a pony at home and would often be collected from school by her father's chauffeur in a black shining car. Monica and I were usually competing for the best marks in class. Sometimes she would lend me special textbooks, but only because her parents told her to. Whenever she could, she showed me utter contempt.'

Sundari looked up.

'Do I bore you with these childish reminiscences?'

'Not at all', Jim replied. 'I'm sorry Ireland treated you so badly.'

'Not Ireland', she said. 'I loved the country. But some of its people can be awfully hard . . . . '

TWENTY

'I don't know why the memory of Monica disturbs me still. Perhaps she embodied at the time all the hostility I experienced as a child: her rejection of me because I was Indian, her contempt for my religion, her attempts to stamp on me whenever she got a chance. And she had all the advantages.

'I remember one occasion when she really hurt me deeply.

'There were rather few Hindus in Dublin, but once in a while we would gather in the house of a prominent person, Mr. Subramanyam, who was press officer in the Indian Embassy. This time it was the feast of Ganesha Chaturthi. Ganesh is the god of wisdom and prosperity. It's a great feast especially for children. After the function sweets and delicacies are handed round, games are organised and everybody is really happy.

'Subramanyam's house was in Rathgar as it happened, not far from the place where Monica's parents had their mansion. At the beginning of the feast *bhajans* are sung in front of the idol. The god looks funny because he carries the head of an elephant, but he is considered kind and generous. The statue is garlanded. *Tilak* is put on its forehead. *Arati* is offered. Then everyone present takes some of the sacrificial food, the *prasad*, that stands before the idol.

'For Hindus all this is just a prayer for prosperity. To outsiders it looks archaic and funny. Would you believe it? Halfway through the function Monica and Mat, her boy friend at the time, gained entrance on some pretext or other and saw what went on. They had even brought a camera with them and made snapshots of the pooja. They disappeared again before I had noticed them.

'A few days later, during religion class, Monica played her

card. It wasn't difficult for her to manipulate the teacher, Sister Eileen, for Eileen had favourites and Monica was number one.

'Monica put up her hand.

"Is worshipping a statue idolatry?' she asked.

"Worshipping a statue is idolatry if one gives it adoration as we should give to God', Eileen replied.

"Is idolatry a mortal sin?' Monica asked again.

"If people do it consciously, yes', Eileen replied. 'Why do you ask?'

"Some people in Dublin commit idolatry', Monica said.

"I don't think so,' Eileen replied. 'You're not referring to veneration of Our Lady, I hope?'

"No', Monica said. 'I'm referring to real idolatry. I saw it and made some photographs of it. May I show them?'

"Yes', Eileen said, unsure of what Monica was up to.

'Monica handed some to Eileen, some to the others in class. They began to point and laugh. Small wonder, because I was on the photographs, bowing to Ganesh . . . .

'As soon as I discovered what she was doing, I packed up my things and walked out of the classroom.

"Stay!', Eileen called after me. 'I'm sure this is a misunderstanding.'

'But I walked out and kept walking till I arrived home. I went to bed and cried my heart out to the despair of my mother whom I refused to tell what was going on.

'That evening a whole delegation from school arrived at our flat to make amends. There was Monica who offered her excuses as she had been told to do. 'I didn't mean to hurt you', she said. But I knew she jolly well had. Eileen was there who was more sincere in her apologies and Sister Pasqualina, the Principal, who promised it would never happen again.

'I needed the whole night to decide whether I would go back to school or not. I felt so humiliated that I doubted whether I could ever face my classmates again. But then I thought of my mother, how my leaving school would break her heart. In my anger I vowed I would always remain a Hindu and destroy

Christianity if I could. And next morning I gritted my teeth and ran the gauntlet of smiles, whispers and contemptuous glances.

'Most of the others were quite decent really. They knew that I'd been treated unfairly. But Monica felt she'd got a knife into me. Sometimes, even weeks later, she would draw her hand over her nose, to remind me of Ganesh, and stick out her tongue. It was then that I decided to take revenge.

'I'm not a violent person by nature, but when I'm wounded I can be as ferocious as a tigress that has lost her cubs. I allowed my anger to make me cold and bitter inside. I made up my mind to wait for the right opportunity, and then to deal Monica the severest blow I could. It's difficult for me now to imagine the hatred I felt. It brought inner darkness. And yet it intoxicated me with its own sweetness and excitement.

'My day dreams were filled with revenge. I contemplated bribing some strong men to beat her up. I considered poisoning her pony, even setting fire to her parents' home. I knew I needed to be more subtle. I also wanted it to be a perfect crime so that I would not get the backlash of incrimination and punishment. I had to protect my mother too. Basically, of course, I was very weak and deprived of the usual resources of crime. I had to rely utterly on cunning.

'My chance came some months later. Monica had been selected to act the prestigious part of Our Lady at the school's Christmas play. Success in this meant a lot to Monica. Her parents and other relatives, as well as all the staff and pupils of the school, would be present. Monica was seeing a lot of her boyfriend Mat during this time, sometimes even on the school grounds; usually in a shed for garden tools at the other end of the playing field. I observed them carefully without giving away my interest.

'Mat worked as an apprentice in a furniture workshop. The surreptitiousness surrounding their meetings convinced me that the friendship was frowned upon by the family. Nor would it be welcomed by the school. Mat and Monica had worked out a system of communication through short written notes which they left in a small crack on the outside of the school building.

'At first I'd thought of disrupting this flow of messages. Then it came to me, in the best tradition of spy catching, that I would profit more from monitoring them carefully. I learned a lot about their habits. I memorised the phrases they used and cracked their simple code. I copied their handwriting till I could imitate it fairly accurately.

'I too was given a part in the Christmas play: as one of the three kings visiting Bethlehem -- the dark one, of course. I accepted, because it fitted well in my plan.

'I made all my preparations, but the execution could only begin on the day of the Christmas play itself. The play was supposed to start at half past eight in the evening. At five I checked the crack and found a message from Monica to Mat telling him to meet her after the play. I had expected something of the kind. I replaced it with a faked message in Monica's hand stating: *'Hiroshima. ooo bombers dirty gs.'* Translated it meant: 'Extremely urgent. Meet me at seven thirty in the garden shed.'

'As I had hoped, Mat came along, took the message, scribbled one of his own and left. I picked it up. It confirmed that he would come. I took it away. I put in a faked message in Mat's hand stating: *'Hiroshima, Hiroshima. ooo bombers dirty gs.'*

'At seven most of the pupils acting in the Christmas play had already come. Monica was one of the last. She was dropped off in her father's limousine. Perhaps, because she was late or did not expect a message, she did not check on the crack. This was a blow to my scheme because it was essential for her to go to the garden shed.

'I quickly adopted another plan. I took the message from the crack, put it in an empty Christmas envelope I had with me, walked to the classroom where dressing for the play had begun and dropped the envelope on the large blue shawl and other pieces of outfit labelled 'Our Lady'. Monica came a little later, saw the envelope, opened it and frowned reading the message. I could see the doubt on her face. She looked round. I studiously avoided her glance, bending down as if I were untying my shoes.

'She looked at her watch and shook her head. Then, she turned round and walked out. She had taken the bait!

'A lot of activity was already going on in the school by this time and it was not difficult for me to follow her unnoticed. She took the key to the garden shed, went outside, crossed the playing field in the dark, opened the shed and waited inside. I did not dare to cross the field; I skirted around it along the hedge, confident I would not be seen. I hid myself behind the shed. By now it was half past seven. Then I heard footsteps. Mat had come! He opened the door of the shed. There was a whispered exchange of greetings.

'This was the moment of action. With trembling hands I took a padlock out of my pocket which I had got ready for the purpose. I pushed the door shut from the outside, slid the safety bar over it and secured it with the padlock. They had heard the noise. They started banging on the door . . . . With my heart in my throat I ran back across the field, walked to the dressing room and began putting on my dress. I was just in time. The make-up people wanted to work on us as soon as possible.

'A quarter of an hour later Monica's absence was noticed.

'Sister Eileen, who was in charge of the play, asked anxiously: 'Has anyone seen Monica?'

"She was here ten minutes ago.'

"Where did she go?'

"Don't know.'

"Perhaps she's in the toilet?'

'At a quarter past eight Eileen rang Monica's home. They confirmed that she'd left an hour before. They were just leaving for the play, they said. Eileen was getting into a real state.

"How can she do this to us! We've to start in ten minutes' time!'

'All toilets and classrooms were searched.

'Eileen had been so confident of Monica's presence that no one had been prepared as an understudy. No Monica, no play. Moreover, fears were now mounting that something dreadful might have happened to her. The whole school was in turmoil. The parents, who were now on the scene, demanded that the police be called in. These came ten minutes later. Search parties were organised. One of them heard the banging in the garden shed. Monica was found with Mat.

'The final episode carried all the drama of public shame I had wanted them to have. Monica was dishevelled, and incoherent with guilt and confusion. Her mother scolded her in view of the whole school. Sister Pasqualina cancelled the Christmas play saying such a disgrace had never happened in the school's history. Of course everybody knew Monica had been set up; still they blamed her for meeting with Mat.

'I didn't feel triumphant as I thought I would. I suddenly felt very empty. All the excitement of working out my vengeance had now fallen flat. But I also felt something else I'd never felt before: disgust with myself. I had been vicious and mean, and no amount of justification could change that fact.

'That night I wept again and this time I told my mother everything. She cried with me. She did not blame me or tell me off. She just held me and cried. 'I don't want you to ever nurture hatred', she said.

'My mother was a very good woman, steeped in the *Bhagavadgita*. 'Hatred is not from God', she said. 'Hatred is the cause of all rebirth. Only forgiveness brings peace of mind.' She made me promise that one day I would make peace with Monica. I pleaded with her. She insisted: 'Not now. Not immediately. One day you must apologise to her and make peace.'

'Wow', Jim said, after Sundari had been silent for some time. 'But if you felt so harassed as a girl, how did you ever become a Catholic and a nun?'

'That's another dramatic story', she said, 'that's to say: dramatic for me. Don't you think I'm talking too much about myself?'

'Not at all', Jim assured her.

'After high school I went to college', Sundari mused. 'Teachers Training College. It was during my final year there that my mother died.'

TWENTY ONE

'I was much older then, of course, but I was as fond of her as ever. I needed her emotionally. There was really no one else I could lean on. I had some relatives in Ireland on my father's side but they had always kept at a distance. They disapproved of mixed marriages and never accepted my mother.

'It was very sad really that my mother should die right then. Hardly a year later I would start my first paid job and our circumstances would have improved. As it was she died of pneumonia. It was no more than a neglected cold which got worse before our GP took note. I was devastated. It seemed the end of everything.

'My mother was cremated according to Hindu custom. I knew that would have been her wish. Some representatives of the Indian community were there. A <u>purohit</u> said prayers. There were hardly any flowers. I couldn't afford them and we had no friends to send them. From my father's side no one bothered to come. My only consolation was that some of my fellow students turned up and among them, believe it or not, was Monica.

'Monica and I had joined the TTC together and were still in the same class. I studiously avoided her company and she did the same with regard to me. Seeing her at my mother's cremation shook me. It also reminded me of the promise I had made that one day I would make up to Monica. It seemed as if my mother, from her bier, was urging me: 'Don't wait! Do it now!'

'After the ceremony, when people came up to me to express their condolences, I came face to face with Monica.

"I'm so sorry about your mother's death', she said.

"Thank you', I said. 'Monica, I must talk to you some time.'

"Why not come to my flat?' she replied. As soon as she entered college, her parents had procured her her own student's digs because it was more convenient.

"I will come', I said. 'But I want you to know that it was I who set you up at that Christmas play. I'm sorry about it now.'

"I knew all along that it was you', Monica said. 'Do come and we'll talk it over.'

'A few days later, in her flat, she told me what I'd never known: that my mother herself had gone to see Monica and her parents to ask forgiveness. She had also told them a lot about my problems. She had asked them not to involve the school authorities and to see to it that the whole matter was dropped.

"Your mother really impressed me', Monica said. 'She was a peaceful person and she brought so much peace to us on that Christmas day.'

'I remembered all my mother had said to me, quoting from the *Bagavadgita*. It confirmed what had gradually grown on me as a personal conviction: that our revenge, hatred and violence destroy ourselves and that only peace and love pay off in the end. This is, perhaps, why I'm telling you all this. Our discussion on violence reminded me of the lessons I had to learn in my own life.

'Anyway, my meeting Monica on that evening was the beginning of something I would have considered utterly impossible until that time: getting to know her on a personal basis. In fact, when I found it difficult to stay on in my mother's place, Monica offered me a room in her flat for the rest of that year. It was attractive to me, both as a practical solution and as a challenge to my will to be reconciled.

'I accepted on condition we would share the cost of the flat equally.

"We'll share the cost of food, gas and electricity', she said. 'The rest is on me.'

'And that's how it was. On the remnants of my mother's

pension I could not afford anything more.

'Sharing life with Monica was quite a revelation to me. With all the friends coming to see her all the time, each and every day brought new action and excitement. It also introduced me to a charismatic prayer group that used to meet in her place. I knew a lot about Catholicism, of course, from having attended religious classes and functions in school, but this was different. For the first time I met young men and women who talked openly about their faith. Belief in God meant something to them. It made them happy, exuberant, different. It made me long for the same experience myself. In fact, it made me envy Monica's good fortunes in a new way: in spite of all my good intentions I've never been able to rid myself totally from my childhood urge to rival and outdo Monica!

'I didn't become a Christian that year though. After finishing my teacher's degree, I got a job in a primary school in Ballymcnoon on the outskirts of Dublin. It was there that I met Ryan.

'I had my own little place by then, close to the school. Ryan was an art teacher. How shall I describe him? I'm sure I'm biased because I fell in love with him.

'He had black hair and a boyish face. He was twenty-five, but looked like a teenager. He lived on dreams. He didn't talk much. His power of expression lay in his hands with which he could draw and model and paint. I was having a hard time trying to cope with the unruly brats of Ballymcnoon. After a day's hard struggle Ryan would cheer me up by taking me to the pub and making me laugh.

'We fell in love. Whenever we could we would go for walks in the country side. Ireland is such a beautiful country. We could walk endlessly up a hill and down a valley, across a brook and into a glen, enjoying the rocks and the green and the ever changing landscape. There were days we would walk for hours without saying a word, just holding each other by the hand. It was exhilarating and filled me with unspeakable happiness.

'Ryan wrote poems for me. Some I remember by heart.
Don't fear, my darling, the dark of the cloud

137

that hangs on the hazy horizon
the grumble of thunder
the frightening lightning
the wind that whips the trees bare of branches.
They never can ever
invade our glade
where trust is the trade,
where peace gives us shade.

'Ryan used to kiss me at times. Once on the crest of a hill with a magnificent view he made me sit next to him on a patch of grass. We both looked at the panorama in silent wonder. After a while he turned to me, took me by both hands, looked into my eyes and said: 'I love you.'

'He was so serious that it almost made me afraid.

"I love you too', I said.

'He pressed me to the ground and rolled over on top of me. He kissed me gently again and looked at me with his wide, brown eyes.

"Will you marry me?"

"I don't know', I said. 'You're a Catholic and I'm a Hindu.'

"Won't you become a Catholic for me?"

'I didn't know what to answer. Later I told him I would need to think about it. 'I would never become a Catholic just to marry someone', I said.

'Characteristically, he didn't reply. We continued our trip as if nothing had happened.

'A few months afterwards I contacted the local priest. There wasn't much instruction I needed. I was baptised in a ceremony at which only Ryan and a few friends attended. Monica couldn't come because she had entered the novitiate of a missionary congregation.

'Ryan asked me again if I would marry him. I said 'Yes'. We kept our plans secret for some time, but when the staff of the school came to know it was great news. They wouldn't hear of keeping it simple. They insisted on involving the whole school. Meanwhile family problems began to cloud the horizon.

'Ryan had taken me to his parents once, out in County

138

Kerry. They were polite to me, but after I had gone they put a lot of pressure on Ryan to drop me. Their pressure increased when our marriage plans were announced. I had no inkling of what was going on because Ryan never told me.

On the day of the wedding the whole school was in church. Our principal had agreed to give me away and take my father's place. After I'd put on my bridal dress my heart was singing with joy. I had decided to put all the small problems out of my mind and make the most of my happiness with Ryan.

'Do you know? He never turned up. Simply left me there waiting for him, with all the school to witness my upset and embarrassment . . . .

'Later I found out that the cajoling by Ryan's family had prevailed. They had intimidated and bribed Ryan; and Ryan wasn't really the person to stand up to them. I can't describe the humiliation and sadness I went through. I couldn't understand how anyone I had trusted so much could let me down so badly.

'Now I have come to realise that the break-up may have saved me. Obviously my relationship to Ryan wasn't really mature. We couldn't talk as husband and wife should be able to talk. Our marriage would have foundered on the rocks anyway.

'I don't know why I'm telling you all this. Perhaps it's because I saw you weeping in church and I felt you must have suffered in your life as I have done. Or perhaps our discussion on violence sparked it off. I rarely talk about myself, especially to strangers.'

'I don't feel a stranger any more', Jim said.

'Nor do I', Sundari stated. 'In spite of your tough talk I feel I can trust you.'

'How did you become a nun?' Jim asked.

'I ran straight from the frustrated wedding to the novitiate', she said laughing. 'No, jokes apart, I never thought I would ever want to enter religious life, not after meeting some of the Sisters who taught me.

'The idea came to me in India itself.

'To get Ryan out of my system, I decided to visit India. I could do two things in one stroke: look up Monica who was doing a course as a Junior Sister in Bombay and renewing the ties with my mother's side of the family in Poona. All my Indian relatives are Hindus. While I was with them, I began to ask myself: 'What have I done for my own people?'

'In Monica's convent I met an Australian Sister who was working in the slums around Bombay. She took Monica and myself on a grand tour round the first-aid clinics she had set up. I was impressed by her personality and dedication. It made me want to do something similar myself, in the line of my own field: education.

'I realised that it was the real illiterates, the country folk outside the cities, who would benefit most from my vocation as a teacher. Being a Sister would give me the organisational and spiritual back-up to be really efficient. So I joined the congregation, survived a stormy novitiate, and was appointed to Yuddhapalli. I've never regretted my decision ever since. Although the people can be difficult at times and life tough, I find I can make myself useful in a way I could never have done as a married person.'

Sundari and Jim continued to sit on the side of the river in silence. Their mutual sharings had established a strange new level of intimacy. Jim was happy to have found someone he could talk to and sensed that Sundari too enjoyed his company, in spite of the sharp words they had exchanged earlier.

Suddenly Sundari said: 'I hear voices on the other side of the river.'

She stood up, put her finger to her lips and motioned Jim to follow her. They walked about forty yards downstream and, coming round a tree, saw a man and woman embracing each other on the other side of the small river. They were Paddy and Kameswari. They lay on the grass, holding each other tight and kissing passionately. Jim and Sundari drew back behind the tree. Making as little noise as they could they retraced their steps to the village.

'Your son is a fast worker', Sundari observed.

'How can I stop him?' Jim said.

'If you don't, there will be trouble.'

'Why?'

'Kameswari was my pupil in school. I know her well and can't help hearing rumours about her. One thing that seems certain is that an old colonel, called Pattabhi Raghava Rao, has his eye on her. He too is a native of this village. Some people even maintain that he has already secretly married her. He is a powerful and vindictive man. If he gets to know that she had an affair with your son, he won't stand idly by.'

It gave Jim a lot to think about.

TWENTY TWO

Colonel Rao came to Yuddhapalli a few days later. He stayed with his brother, a few houses down from the Yeddanapudi residence, and invited Jim and Paddy for supper there. He was his usual cheerful and talkative self.

After having offered an excellent meal, with plenty of beer and gin, Rao introduced a new topic.

'Tonight we are going to a neighbouring village to attend a burrakatha party.'

'What is that?'

'A burrakatha is a traditional epic sung and recited by three singers. Most of the narration is done by the main singer who has a phenomenal memory, for the performance lasts for many hours. He is assisted by the other two who sing refrains and accompany him with drums.'

'The language they use is Telugu, I suppose?'

'Indeed. You'll not be able to follow the contents. The reason I am taking you there is that I would like you to meet the main burrakatha singer, Beela Hanumantha Rao. He is a friend of mine, a visionary who wants to liberate the poor people from their oppressors.'

'Does he do that by singing his songs?'

'To begin with, yes. He has a tremendous influence on the people. But he is more than a preacher. He is the head of an active Naxalite group.'

'You must excuse our ignorance', Jim said. 'But who on earth are Naxalites?'

'They are communist activists who believe the time has come to take up arms in the struggle for liberation. They owe their name to the fact that in 1964 they killed a rich landowner and his family in the village of Naxalbari. The man owned 10,000 acres of land and had kept thousands of landless labourers in abject poverty.'

'What does the Government of India think about them?'

'The Naxalites have been persecuted from the beginning, understandably so. I too believe they should be treated with caution, though they come in useful at times . . . . . Most of the original leaders have been caught and are in prison for life. Beela is one of the few who has kept going until now. In fact, apart from his close friends, no one knows that he is the brain behind the Naxalites in this district.'

Jim did not particularly look forward to meeting the rebel leader. He suspected Rao was trying to implicate them in some devious scheme.

It was a scene Jim would never forget. On an open field outside the village they had driven to, more than a thousand workers had gathered. Wrapped in their blankets they were sitting in a wide circle round an improvised stage where the three singers, in their colourful traditional costumes, were giving the performance. Because of the powerful floodlight in front of their feet they could be seen from a great distance. Loudspeakers had been provided which carried their voices far beyond the heads of the spectators into the village.

Jim, Paddy, Rao and some local dignitaries were sitting on chairs in a place of honour. Jim watched people's faces and was impressed by their intense participation. Sometimes they reflected anger, hatred or fear. Then again they lit up in smiles or in boisterous laughter. It was a preacher's dream: instruction mixed with popular entertainment.

'What is the story?' Jim asked Rao.

'The main story is about a Muslim king, Tughlag, who becomes rich by oppressing people in a hundred ways. But the people have their own tricks to deceive him. Eventually they lure him into a trap and finish him off.'

'Brilliant.'

'The main story is laced with humorous asides and anecdotes. Beela will suddenly interrupt the main flow by narrating a present-day tale: an incident or example that links people's actual lives to the traditional narration.'

'Could you give an example?'

'Certainly. He has just spoken of the case of a road contractor whom he claims to know, who is a genius in getting money. The government pays him for constructing a road between two villages. He convinces the village panchayats that he needs to bribe the government to get the road sanctioned. So they offer him a donation. For the benefit of giving them employment, he takes a one rupee bribe per day from each of the labourers who work for him. He gets the merchants in the villages to supply free lorries to cart stones, in exchange for their being allowed to use the road later on. The only reason why he eventually stops making money on the road is, according to Beela, the simple fact that nobody has any money left and that he can now move his operation to another set of villages.'

'Small wonder that they enjoy it', Jim said.

At the end of the performance, while people were drifting home, Rao introduced Beela to Jim and Paddy. Beela , naked from his waist up, was bending over a bucket of water to wash the make-up from his face. He was a strong and muscular man. He eyed the two newcomers speculatively. His command of English proved to be elementary.

'Happy you here', he said. With a firm, wet grip, he shook hands.

Beela then began to speak Telugu with Rao. The two men obviously knew each other well. It looked as if they were negotiating a deal.

'In exchange for your help in the future, he's offering you protection', Rao said.

'Why would we need protection?', Jim asked.

'He's got followers everywhere. You're not safe without his protection.'

'I thought we were your friends.'

'Of course. But it's better not to argue with him. Accept his protection'.

'But I don't want to make any promises. I've no intention of getting involved in a local Armageddon'.

'Of course not. I will see to that.'

Rao spoke again to Beela who nodded. There was hand-shaking all around and they left.

Jim was unhappy with the situation but he did not know how to extricate himself now. Perhaps all they could do was play along for the time being.

They drove back through the night in Rao's Landrover. Coming round a bend in the road, they found the way barred by a police block. An officer stood in the middle. Constables on either side of the road trained rifles on the car.

'Don't worry', Rao said. 'This is a routine search. They're looking for arms.'

It reminded Jim, with a shock, of the roadblocks he had been used to in Ireland.

They were told to leave the car. Police constables frisked them. They searched the Landrover from top to bottom. When the officer was satisfied that there were no guns, he began to interrogate Rao. Rao spoke to him, first softly, then in ever more vehement tones. Eventually they were allowed to get back into the car and continue their journey.

'What did he want from you?' Jim asked.

'He wanted to know what two Europeans were doing in this part of Andhra Pradesh. It is somewhat unusual, of course. He may have thought that you were agents from a communist country. I had to tell him that you are staying in Yuddhapalli. I'm sure he will send some detectives tomorrow to find out about you.'

Next day Rao looked up Jim in his room in the guest bungalow. Jim could see that the colonel was agitated.

'You are the person in charge! You are responsible!'

'What are you talking about?' Jim wanted to know.

'There are rumours in the village that your man is taking
liberties with Kameswari.'

'What kind of liberties?' Jim asked to stall for time.

'He takes her for walks, holding her hand. He's breaking his
code as a guest. He should respect the lady in whose house he
lives.'

'Surely Kameswari knows what she's doing. She's old
enough.'

'She's been silly. I'll talk to her. But you have to talk to him
too.'

'Why?'

'Do you want him to get involved in a scandal? The whole
village will talk about the two of you.'

'I see.'

'You must stop him.'

'If I can. But it may not be possible . . . . Then there's
another thing I'd like to point out. Sometimes the more
pressure you exert the more you may be driving people
together. If they feel we are all against their friendship, they
may enjoy it as a challenge all the more.'

'You don't really want to help me', Rao said.

'On the contrary. What I'm trying to say is: sometimes we
achieve our objective better by strategy than by force.'

Rao thought about this.

Then he said to Jim: 'Listen to this. I am in love with
Kameswari. If I ever were to find out that your man sleeps with
her, I would kill him and you too.'

Shaking with anger, he rose from his seat and left the room.

TWENTY THREE

Jim had been wondering how to reopen contact with Sundari. Would she be embarrassed if he would drop in to see her at the convent some evening? She was the only person in the village he could fully trust, he knew; and, he admitted to himself, he found her an attractive companion. His brooding was resolved three days later when he received a message from her. Could he come to see her at the high school around four o'clock? He almost jumped with excitement. She herself had made the next move!

He presented himself a quarter of an hour early at the school entrance. A clerk in the office gave him a chair to sit on till the end-of-class bell was rung. As in schools all over the world this brought about a veritable eruption. Suddenly swarms of children emerged from the classrooms and surged through the main corridor toward the entrance. Jim hastily retreated to the office where Sundari came to liberate him.

'Let's go to the parlour. We need to talk.'

Seeing her, cheerful and bright as ever, made his pulse beat faster with anticipation. But any hope of her seeking more than business was dashed by her briskness.

'I don't have a lot of time', she said as soon as they had sat down in the school's reception room. 'I've heard rumours that upset me.'

'More small talk about Paddy and Kameswari?'

'More serious than that.'

'What about?'

'Next week the District Collector, who's the highest government official in this area, will come to the village to open the new branch of the Podcham irrigation scheme. Of course, it's a political stunt engineered by our panchayati president,

Madhura. It's his way of crowning a pretty nasty piece of wheeling and dealing.'

'In what way?'

'When the canal was being planned, Madhura saw to it that the new channels would benefit his own fields and those of his fellow Reddies rather than those of the rival farmers, the Kammas. By the prospect of regular water supply his own land has increased at least four times in value. As if he weren't rich enough.'

'Shrewd lad.'

'Not half. But that's no news. Everybody knows and most people in the village hate his guts.'

'What's the news?'

'There's a persistent rumour that something is going to happen and that there will be a big fight.'

'Between the Reddies and Kammas?'

'That's not clear. As principal of the school I have friends among the pupils and their parents. From the information I've received I gather that the harijans, the Malas and the Madigas, will also be involved.'

'Is the information not specific?'

'No.'

'How do you know then there will be a fight?'

'Well, some of the girls have told me that three feathers of a dead crow have been passed from house to house in the Madiga quarter. It's a kind of coded sign. Crows are associated with unwelcome visitors - which might point to the coming of the District Collector. The three feathers indicate the third quarter of the moon. It tallies with the date of the function. Feathers are what remain after a cat kills a bird. Through this kind of action people are mentally prepared to get ready for a fight.'

'Why tell me?' Jim said.

'I would advise you to leave the village before then.'

'Nothing doing. We've come for a long stay.'

Sundari looked at him speculatively.

'All right, I'll come clean with you if you promise to do the same.'

'If I can', Jim said cautiously.

'You've come to our village in order to attend the function, haven't you?'

'Come off it! Certainly not. This is the first time I heard of it.'

'I don't believe you. In fact, I've reasons to think that you've something to do with the clash people are expecting.'

'Utter nonsense! How could we? I tell you: this is the first time I've heard of the District Collector and, in fact, the first time I've heard the word 'district collector'. If you hadn't explained the term to me, I'd have thought he is some kind of stamp collector or garbage collector. What makes you think we're involved, anyway?'

'Crow feathers are black. Two white diagonal lines had been painted on the feathers. Since you are two white men who've only appeared recently in the village, people interpret the lines as a pointer to you.'

'Ridiculous', Jim protested.

'Not ridiculous. People are quite shrewd and whoever codes these messages makes sure they get the point. If you don't know anything about it, it's very strange indeed.'

'I really don't', Jim said.

He thought for a moment.

'Who is masterminding this whole business? Who's hyping the people up by sending those messages?'

'I wish I knew.'

'Don't people know?'

'I suppose they do, or at least some of them. But the children don't. There are some secret, revolutionary organisations in this area. They are usually the ones to stir up trouble.'

'I see', Jim said. A picture was beginning to emerge: Beela Hanumantha Rao, the Naxalite! Beela was the kind of man who could well be stirring up the trouble . . . . But what on earth could Paddy and he have to do with it?

'Sundari', he said. 'Thank you for telling me what you have done. I don't understand what it's all about but I'll make sure

149

we're on our guard.'

'You better be', she said, 'also for the sake of our village.'

'So?'

'We've had violence and bloodshed before. It always leads to further violence and bloodshed. Please, spare our people.'

'I assure you I've no intention at all in getting involved in any conflict over here. We've got too much of it at home. I'm not a warmonger, you know.'

'I'm ready to believe you', she said, looking into his eyes with an unusual seriousness. 'I cannot fully make sense of you, but I'm sure I can trust you. Sorry, if I've upset you.'

Jim felt awkward. He would have loved to blurt it all out: his involvement with the ILF and the dreadful events which had forced him to take refuge in India. She was the one person who would listen, he knew, and not reject him outright. But he suppressed the urge. He would have to carry his burden alone . . . .

They went onto the flat roof of the school building. It was from there that they saw the woman being followed. The rest was traumatic: his encounter with the harassed woman, his fight with the men in Pothamma's shrine, his agonising prayer as he knelt beside her drowned and lifeless body.

It was only Sundari's gentle, but firm prompting that finally made him return to the Yeddanapudi home.

Back in his own room, Jim had a bath and stretched out on his bed to take stock of the situation. He was still badly shaken by the violence he had witnessed that afternoon. He also recalled what Sundari had told him. It all seemed to make a pattern: the 'job' Rao kept talking about, their meeting with the Naxalite leader, the rumours about the impending fight. But he could not make head or tail of it. One thing he knew: some individuals were going to try to use Paddy and himself for their own devious ends. He was not going to let it happen.

150

Should he tell Paddy?

Perhaps not. He could not be absolutely sure that Paddy would not spill the beans to Kameswari and Jim knew she must somehow be in the plot . . . .

Later that evening Paddy and Jim were sitting on the verandah of their little bungalow drinking a glass of beer. Jim had recounted the fate of the unfortunate woman. Paddy was genuinely shocked -- all the more so because of his involvement with Kameswari, Jim thought.

Then, with his usual brusque manner, Paddy dismissed the whole affair, produced a simple bamboo flute and began to blow on it.

Paddy had seen a boy in the village play the flute and had bought it off him. He mastered it remarkably well, sometimes playing traditional Irish tunes, sometimes inventing melancholy melodies of his own.

'Nice', Jim said. 'You've got talent.' He meant it.

'I used to play the mouth organ when I was a kid', Paddy answered. 'I like playing.'

'You're good at it. When we come back home you can give a concert in the local pub.'

Paddy played on for a while. Jim listened to the music and reflected on how little he knew Paddy. Probably he was like so many people he knew: rough on the outside but capable of a deep tenderness as well.

'Are you still staying with your parents?' Jim asked when Paddy seemed to have exhausted his repertoire.

Paddy shrugged his shoulders. 'So what?'

'Do you have a job?'

Paddy shook his head.

Jim was not surprised. He knew that among youngsters of Paddy's age in Catholic areas unemployment can be as high as fifty per cent . . . .

'Did you train for anything?'

'I worked as a motor mechanic, then as a courier on a motorbike.'

'What are the things you like doing? Any special hobbies?'

Paddy looked at him as if to test Jim's interest. Satisfied, he shrugged his shoulders again and said: 'I build ships in bottles.'

'You what?'

'I build ships, miniature sailing boats and so on.'

'How do you get them into a bottle?'

'That's quite an art. You need some special tweezers for that. Whatever you're building is in small parts. You push them in one by one and fiddle around till they fit. It takes a lot of patience.'

'Incredible!' Jim said. 'I've seen them sometimes in shops and have always wondered how they are put together. When did you take this up?'

'A long time ago. A great uncle of mine used to stay with my grand dad. They were brothers you see. He used to work on these bottles and he showed me how to do it. I picked it up from him.'

'Good for you. Why don't you do one here?'

'I wouldn't mind . . . . I'd have to make my own tools . . . '

Jim woke up in the middle of the night. Outside his door a stool had fallen on the floor making a sharp noise. Jim sat bolt-upright. An intruder. He himself had carefully balanced the stool against the door in such a way that the least disturbance would topple it.

He heard no further noise. Whoever it was must be holding his breath, waiting for a response.

Jim got up as silently as he could, put on his trousers and a shirt and moved to the door. No sound. He decided to follow the strategy he had previously thought out for such an eventuality.

He moved over to the window, unlocked the wooden shutters, pushed them open and looked outside. Since his eyes were adjusted to darkness, he could see quite well in the faint light of the half moon. He could make out nothing unusual.

Silently he opened the shutters a little more, swung his legs over the sill and jumped off on the other side. He hoped the soft thud of his feet on the sand had not been heard. Wrong. They had. A shadow moved from the front of the bungalow and ran across the compound to the gate.

Jim ran after him. The man, who was wrapped in a blanket, turned left into the street. Jim followed him. He blessed the faint moonlight. With its many potholes the track was treacherous.

There was little noise apart from the soft patter of their two pairs of feet. A dog barked in a house they passed. Jim cursed when he hurt his foot on a sharp stone. He realised it would be hard for him to outrun the Indian with bare feet.

The man turned into some small alleys. Suddenly he had disappeared. Jim walked around for a while but knew he had lost him. He turned back to the Yeddanapudi home, climbed back into his room, took off his clothes and went back to bed.

Next morning Paddy knocked on his door.

'See what we've got for breakfast', he said.

Jim came out and saw a small net hanging from the roof over the verandah. It contained an assortment of odds and ends: a green chilly, a lemon, an onion and the chopped-off head of a chicken.

One of the servant girls saw it too. She shrieked with terror, calling the whole household together.

A neighbour explained to Jim and Paddy that it could bring bad luck.

'It's a curse and a warning', he said.

Velamma, Kameswari's mother, was visibly upset. She summoned a Brahmin to performed a *pooja* in the compound. Sanskrit slokas were recited. The magical objects were destroyed in a fire.

'Somebody doesn't like us', Paddy said.

Many relatives and friends of the Yeddanapudis attended

the purification rite. Jim realised that news of the incident would spread to the whole village. Was this another ploy to incite tension and fear?

TWENTY FOUR

It was almost a relief when Rao and Kameswari turned up two days later with business on their minds. Jim sensed it from the way they tried to ingratiate themselves. He knew that the special lunch prepared with food they had brought with them from Hyderabad was just a prelude.

Sure enough, at the end of the meal, Rao had the table cleared and produced from his briefcase a map which he spread on the table.

'This is a map of the village', he said.

It was a rough sketch which he had drawn himself. After indicating some of the well-known landmarks, he came to the point.

'This here is a new canal that branches off from the Podcham irrigation project. It could improve our crops enormously if the water were divided equally among all the farmers. Madhura and his Reddy clique have seen to it that the channels run mainly through their lands.'

He indicated where the Reddy fields and the Kamma fields were situated.

'Now after some days the new canal will be officially opened by one of Madhura's friends, the District Collector. It will be a grand occasion to which they hope to give a lot of publicity.'

Here Kameswari took over.

'Rao and I cannot bear the thought of Madhura getting away with it without even a whisper of protest. So we would like to stage a small demonstration.'

'What kind of demonstration?'

'Oh, not a protest march or anything like that. It would not make the slightest impression on our adversaries. We want

155

to do something more spectacular, something that will be remembered.'

'Fireworks!' Paddy said.

'Yes, fireworks of a kind. Now, let me explain what we had in mind.'

She threw an anxious glance at Jim while bending over the map.

'See, here are the sluices of the new canal. The function will take place right in this open area next to the sluices. A stage will be put up. There will be speeches and dances. Then the District Collector will unveil a plaque and the sluices will be opened so that the first water can flow into the channels.'

'So what's the plan?' Paddy asked.

'We want to put an explosive charge inside the dam next to the sluices. We'll work it in such a way that when the District Collector presses the button, the dam will explode.'

'What damage will it do? Will it hurt people?' Jim asked.

'No. It won't hurt people. There will be a sudden flood but it will flow across the fields. It is not strong enough to go beyond the banks or reach the houses of the village. Since Madhura has just planted his paddy, all it will do is destroy his crop. At least, that's what we hope. Instead of it being a moment of triumph, it will be a day of loss and shame.'

Interiorly Jim sighed with relief. He was happy no assault on people was being planned. But he would play hard to get.

'Why talk to us about all this?'

Rao turned on Jim.

'You have already figured that out. The two of you are explosives experts. We want you to help us lay the charge and fix the detonator.'

'Hold on', Jim replied. 'We are not experts and your dislike of Madhura is none of our business. We won't touch the whole scheme with a barge pole.'

'Before you say no, listen', Kameswari said. 'There's absolutely no danger in this for either of you. When we agreed to give you shelter, it was understood you should give us this kind of assistance.'

156

'Nonsense', Jim said tersely. 'We've not been told about any such understanding. In fact, we were told just the opposite: to stay put and keep our hands clean.'

'Most unfortunate', Rao came in. 'There must have been a hitch in your communication. It does happen you know. Anyway, we cannot go back on our agreement. We promised to shield you on some explicit conditions.'

Kameswari looked at Paddy with an appeal in her eyes. He responded.

'I don't see why we can't take it on. If we get the right stuff, it's a doddle.'

'That's not the point', Jim said. 'If we take this on we'll get involved in a fight that's not ours.'

'So what?' Paddy countered. 'Our friends' fight is our own fight. I'm bored stiff. This thing won't harm us. It will be a diversion.'

Jim closed his eyes and thought. He was not going to win this way.

'Let's first clear up a few things', he said. 'A few nights ago someone fixed a charm to our bungalow. It was a curse, I'm told. Who put it there and why?'

Rao hesitated. 'We've heard about it. It was a pretty disgusting thing to do. Kameswari and I believe it was done by the Reddies to scare you off.'

'Rubbish', Jim said. 'Why would the Reddies bother to do a thing like that if they're in control of the situation as you maintain? There's more behind it.'

'Many people in the village are superstitious', Kameswari said. 'They don't like strangers. The Reddies use such feelings to stir people up against us. It's psychological warfare.'

'But if what you say is true, what will people do if they were to find out that the two of us have planted the bomb? You know it's impossible to keep secrets in a village. We'll be held responsible.'

'You'll have nothing to fear', Rao said. 'We'll be well out of reach before Madhura and his club realise what has happened or who is responsible. We're not going to hang around.'

'Where will you get the explosives from?'

'We've got them. All it needs is expert hands to wire them up and set the detonator.'

'Terrific! Let's have a look!' Paddy said.

'No!' Jim said.

'Listen to this', Rao said. 'since you claim to know village people so well. You'll be implicated whether you like it or not. The smallest suspicion in their minds can be turned into a certainty by no more than a whisper. It's safer for you to be on our side.'

It was a threat. Jim knew the man was right. They would be implicated whatever they did. Perhaps it was better to play along and remain somewhat in control of events . . . .

'Paddy and I need to talk', Jim said. 'Alone.'

Jim took Paddy on a walk through the village. He wanted to make sure they could not be overheard.

'What's the problem?' Paddy asked.

'It stinks', Jim replied. 'They're only telling us half the truth. They're dragging us into something messy that may stick to us. Moreover, we did get instructions to keep our noses clean. What will Derry say if we get the police after us? It's something we can't risk.'

'You let your bloody mind run riot', Paddy protested. 'It's not that big. The dam can be repaired soon enough. I think it will be fun.'

'It won't', Jim growled. 'I know we can't trust these bastards.'

'Hang on. Rao may be a bastard. Kameswari isn't. I'd trust her any time. She wouldn't do anything to harm us.'

They walked on in silence.

People from the village greeted them but Jim also had the impression they were being watched with more curiosity than before. Or was it only his fertile imagination seeing things?

158

He came to a decision.

'All right, Paddy, I see you want to give it a go. In the cir
cumstances we can hardly do anything else. You'll be my
witness about it if Derry hauls us over the coals later. We have
no choice. But I want to lay down the terms under which we
will agree to cooperate. You must back me up in everything I
say. Remember, I'm in charge and in things of this nature you
have to obey my orders.'

'Right, boss', Paddy said.

He was genuinely happy that the job was on.

Back in their bungalow the deal was forged.

'We agree to help you on a number of conditions.'

'What conditions?' Rao said.

'If we set the charge, we will keep control of the detonation
till the last moment.'

'OK', Rao replied.

'This will be the last and only job we do for you.'

'Agreed.'

'A vehicle should be ready so that we can leave the village
immediately after the explosion and we'll never return to this
place again.'

'That was already part of our plan', Rao said.

'Finally, I will only give the final go-ahead if I have satisfied
myself fully that no personal harm will come to any individual.'

'No problem. I'll take you round by jeep so that you can see
the terrain for yourself. I agree to all your conditions.'

Kameswari beamed.

'Thank you', she said, looking at Jim and then at Paddy with
a dazzling smile.

Late that evening when the servants had retired Kameswari took Jim and Paddy to her own bedroom in her mother's bungalow.

She carefully closed the doors of the room.

She walked over to a tall steel wardrobe against the back wall. It was heavily padlocked.

'Most farmers have either a steel box or a wardrobe like this', she said. 'to keep money and jewellery. Look at my treasure.'

She unlocked the padlocks and opened the doors. Inside there were two machine guns, hand-grenades, a World War II land mine and row upon row of grey packets: gelignite!

Paddy whistled. 'Enough crackers to send the whole village sky high.'

'I'm glad we don't need all of it', Kameswari said.

TWENTY FIVE

Next day Rao took Kameswari and the two men round in his jeep. They visited the new canal, saw the dam and the sluices. They drove along one of the new channels which cut right through Reddy land. Some fields had already been irrigated. Women workers stood ankle deep in the mud, bending low to plant tender shoots of rice in neatly spaced rows.

'Madhura owns many of these people', Rao growled.

'Owns them?'

'Yes. During a drought or times of famine, he hands out bags of grain to the poor labourers in exchange for future work. Some owe him from five to ten years labour. It's known as bonded labour.'

'Doesn't the government forbid this kind of practice?'

'It does, at least in theory. The problem is that no one dares to defy Madhura publicly by exposing what he does. He bribes the officials who could bring him to court if they wanted to.'

In contrast, the Kamma fields were visibly in a poorer condition. They were far away from the channels. No paddy would grow here; only dry crops such as tobacco, cotton and chilly.

'And these will only yield a harvest if there is enough rain', Kameswari said.

They stopped at a small house belonging to one of Rao's relatives. The owner of the house introduced his family and offered them a cup of coffee.

Rao interpreted his story.

'Until last year I possessed five acres of land. It was my share of my family's patrimony. Three years of crop failure and sickness among my buffaloes made me incur such crippling debts that my creditors demanded I sell the land. Then

161

Madhura intervened. By buying me out, he became the owner and I and my family have become his tenants. If he wants to, he can evict me any time.'

The story touched a sensitive chord in Jim. Was it not through rigorous control of the land that the Protestants in Ireland had maintained ascendancy over the Catholic peasants? He himself had written a small playlet about it, a sketch, during his seminary days. Since the characters and their dialogue were of his own creation, and charged with deep personal feelings, he could recall the text almost word for word.

The play had described the struggle between the people of a small Catholic hamlet, Candarmagh in Country Antrim, and their Protestant landlord. The setting was the potato famine of 1845. Jim had researched the background and ferreted out the available data. He had presented the facts in a dramatic clash between two fictitious protagonists: the honest, hard working Diarmuid O'Flynn, the leading tenant, who kept pleading that the people be fed; and the arrogant Ian McHurd, the landlord, who insisted on selling the crops abroad. O'Flynn's repeated cry: 'Don't let our people die of starvation!' only met the taunt: 'Die, miserable Mary-worshippers! God strikes you for your papist superstitions!'

Jim had written these lines with his blood boiling in his veins. The characters might be imaginary, the facts were not. In 1845 alone 700,000 peasants died of hunger, but mass export of grain and cattle to England continued, to satisfy the greed of English merchants. In five years of starvation and emigration the population dwindled from eight to four and a half millions . . . .

Jim had concluded his sketch like a classical Greek tragedy with scenes of retribution on the threshing floor: O'Flynn handing out measures of wheat to the hungry country folk; McHurd bringing bailiffs to arrest him; a passionate prayer of O'Flynn calling on God to intervene; a bolt of lightning that hit

McHurd and struck him dead.

'I carry in me roots of anger that are centuries deep', Jim thought. *'Perhaps Paddy is right. The fight of these peasants against Madhura Reddy is our fight too. We are providing a bolt of lightning.'*

'The truth of the matter', Sundari stated, in reply to Jim's questions regarding Madhura Reddy, 'the truth of the matter is a little more complex. Madhura may be a scoundrel at times, he is not much worse than the others.

I'm sure what you have heard is the Kamma view, through your staying in the Yeddanapudi home. Their vision is coloured, to say the least. In the past this village was run by the Kammas. The low-caste workers were equally oppressed, if not more so. Their farming methods were primitive. Matters only began to improve when Madhura's grandfather came to the village with some other Reddies. They were immigrants from coastal Andhra, another part of the State. People from this region, which is Telengana, have never forgiven the intrusion, even though the Reddies brought money and new skills.

From the beginning the Kammas resented the success of the Reddies. They harassed them, even assassinated some leaders and burned their houses. Small wonder that the Reddies retaliated and tried to consolidate their position through every possible means.

What we have here is basically a sectarian fight between different interest groups: between Kammas and Reddies, between Andhras and Telenganas, between old residents and immigrants. The bloody clashes of the past are perpetuated by sectarian tales of horror which prepare the younger generation for warfare even before it can make up its own mind. Every fresh act of violence leads to counter-violence and a deepening of the wounds. It's a cyclone of violence that nurtures itself.'

'But surely you don't condone Madhura's exploiting the

163

poor?'

'Of course I don't. Injustice and corruption abound. It's found among the Kammas no less than among the Reddies. The real solution does not lie in favouring one party or the other but in instilling a new attitude in all.'

'And how are you going to do that?'

'We are trying here in our school. I'm teaching girls from all castes. In class, on the playground, in discussion groups I make sure to mix Kammas and Reddies. Genuine friendships develop. The girls are really quite open to forgive and forget and start afresh, if their families at home would allow them to. The same applies to the boys. It's their families that instil the hatred and draw them into the fight.'

'I see.'

Sundari had spoken with deep conviction. She lived what she believed. Her face radiated a calm and a sense of purpose Jim admired and envied. She turned to him and noticed his look. It made her tackle him head on.

'Violence anywhere is not much different from violence in Northern Ireland . . . . '

'So?'

'What we would need is a massive explosion.'

'An explosion?'

'An explosion of love. I've often thought about it. How do you stop cyclones? I once read that scientists plan to blow them out through a nuclear explosion - if the fall-out could be avoided in future technology. It's an image that has stuck to my mind. A cyclone of violence can only be blown out by an explosion of love.'

'A dream', Jim said.

'I don't know.'

'You believe it could really happen?'

'I believe it has begun to happen. I'm not sure how much of a practising Catholic you are, otherwise you'd know what I mean.'

'Try me.'

'I believe it happened in Jesus. His death and resurrection

164

were an explosion of love. It has never stopped healing wounds, bringing people together, creating new communities of love.'

'I wish I had your faith', Jim said.

He meant it.

His mind was on an explosion of a different type.

TWENTY SIX

During the nights Paddy worked on the gelignite in Kameswari's room. Jim stayed around, most of the time. The more he thought about it, the more he regretted having agreed to play along. Why can't I have more backbone, like Sundari? he thought. Or more faith in the power of the Gospel?

Two days before the event labourers were set to work on clearing the site for the function. The field next to the dam was levelled. A make-shift stage was erected. A small triumphal arch was built over the road where it entered the field. It bore the inscription: 'Welcome to our District Collector'. All round the field bamboo poles were planted and linked to each other with ropes that carried buntings and flags. Before the stage a tent covering, a *shamyana*, was to provide shade for the notables and chief guests.

Everything was done as Rao had predicted. He had been well-informed, Jim thought. Madhura himself came once or twice during the day to supervise the proceedings. He even tried out personally the microphone system hired from a nearby town.

Next day during the afternoon Rao convoked a council of war.

'Are the explosives ready?'

Paddy and Kameswari nodded.

'Can we place them tonight?'

'Yes.'

'How much time do you need to set them up?'

'About an hour', Paddy said. 'I've put gelignite into three jerry cans. What we need to do is to dig a hole in the side of the dam. Three to four feet is probably deep enough. One of the jerry cans carries the aerial. To make sure it will pick up the radio signal it should be exposed to the open air. So we'll lead the antenna upwards in a plastic tube that reaches all the way up. We'll put some grass or leaves over it to disguise its top.'

'Great!' Rao said.

'Wait. What about the safeguards?' Jim said.

'Safeguards? Let's talk about that tomorrow morning before the function. Our immediate job now is to get the bomb in place.'

'Will there be people around tonight?'

'There will be. Madhura has appointed four of his labourers to keep watch during the night. It's to stop anybody pilfering or stealing the microphone equipment.'

'How can we get round them?'

'I've been in touch with Beela. He says he'll solve that problem. He's got an enormous hold on these harijans. He'll make them leave the place for a couple of hours.'

'So what's the time schedule?' Kameswari asked.

'If I tell Beela to draw the men away between twelve and two, would that give you enough time?'

'It would.' Paddy said.

'OK. That's how it will be.'

Jim could not suppress his anxiety later that day when Paddy and he were on their own.

'I don't like it a bit', he said.

'So?',

'How do we know there will be no people on the dam?'

'So what?'

'Well, can't you see? There's this big function. People coming to it from far and wide. There may not be enough room in the meeting area. Some people may settle themselves on or near the dam. Or children may get bored with the speeches and play near the bomb. How can we be sure no one gets hurt when you set it off?

'Tough luck,' Paddy replied.

'What?! Tough luck?' Jim almost exploded with rage. 'Are you still human? Do you really want to kill innocent people? What kind of beast are you?'

Paddy looked at Jim with astonishment. He had not expected such an outburst. Jim continued.

'I don't know how to get this into your thick skull. I can understand you hurting someone, or even killing someone, if you're defending your own people. I can't see how you can ever justify hurting innocent people because the Reddies and Kammas of this village are having a fight. Don't you have an ounce of human feeling left in you?'

He went on in a more conciliatory tone.

'Look here, Paddy, I know you're not a bad chap really. Remember the donkey, how you bought her to save her from feeling the wound on her back? Imagine your bomb would make a child blind or rip a leg or an arm off a pretty girl, wouldn't you be sorry?'

It made an impression on Paddy.

'Do you want to stop the whole business?'

'I wish we could', Jim said.

He paced up and down the verandah.

'In the circumstances we'd better go on making all the preparations. But, remember what I told Rao: we will hold on to the detonator. We ourselves will check if everything is safe. Only if we can see that no harm can come to any person, will we activate the detonator. And I am the one to make that final decision. Understood?'

'Yes, boss', Paddy said.

At ten minutes past twelve they were on the site. It was totally deserted, as Rao had promised. Paddy and Jim were carrying the jerry cans, Kameswari a torch and two spades.

They examined the dam. It ran fifty feet across from one

side to the other. It rose approximately eight feet above water level. At the top its width did not exceed three feet but it widened out at the bottom. It had been constructed of pieces of rock covered by sand.

'To make sure we breach it, the charge should be laid just above the waterline', Paddy determined.

He indicated a spot in the middle of the dam on the side facing the water, close to one of the sluices.

They began to dig with energy. It proved a hard job. The stones had to be dislodged one by one, then pulled up. Excavating a hole that could hold the three cans and that was deep enough, took the best part of an hour. The cans were put in position. Stones were piled on top of them, leaving space for the tube that contained the aerial. Then everything was filled in with sand, the extremity of the aerial remaining hidden under a small weed planted there from somewhere else.

They dumped the excess stones into the canal. They covered the place where they had been digging with dirt and dust from the road to remove all traces of their work.

'God help us', Jim thought. 'I'll be relieved when this nightmare is over'.

They arrived back at the Yeddanapudi home without meeting anyone. Jim said good night to Kameswari and Paddy, entered his room and made ready to go to bed.

The two remained on the verandah, whispering for some time. Then Jim heard Paddy's door being opened and closed. He had the distinct impression Kameswari had followed Paddy into his room.

Not being able to contain his curiosity, Jim slipped out onto the verandah, approached Paddy's door and put his ear to it. Indeed! He could hear them talk and giggle. He did not like it but knew it would be futile to interfere.

Half an hour later - Jim was still awake - he heard a soft knock on his door.

He switched on the light and put on his trousers and shirt.

'Who are you?' he asked.

'It's me', Rao whispered from outside.

Jim opened the door and let him in.

'What's the matter? We placed the bomb.'

'I know you have. I'm worried about Kameswari.'

'She was with us till we came back. She must be in her room.'

'She isn't.'

'I wouldn't know where she is', Jim lied.

'I don't know what can have happened to her', Rao said. 'For reasons I can't explain to you, I'm worried. Some enemies may have kidnapped her . . . . '

At that very moment Paddy's door opened and both Jim and Rao could hear how he and Kameswari were taking leave of each other in whispered voices.

Rao became white as a sheet.

He turned round and entered the verandah just in time to see Paddy give Kameswari a parting kiss.

Kameswari shrunk back when she saw him.

'We were preparing for tomorrow', she stammered.

'You, whore!' Rao replied, adding a few stinging words in Telugu that made her cringe.

Then he faced Paddy.

'I warned you. You will regret your misconduct.'

'Calm down!' Paddy said. 'We were only having a friendly chat.'

But Rao had already turned away, walking down the steps that led from the verandah and taking Kameswari with him.

'Pompous old bastard!' Paddy muttered.

But Jim felt uneasy.

While undressing a second time he made up his mind to watch Rao. His threat to Paddy spelled inevitable trouble. Rao was a dangerous man . . . . .

170

TWENTY SEVEN

Early next morning Rao convoked another meeting. Kameswari looked tired as if she had not slept the whole night. Rao was brusque and short, indicating by his manner that he had not forgotten the incident but had decided to let the matter rest for the time being.

'Where's the detonator?' he wanted to know.

'It's with me', Paddy said.

He showed an oblong plastic case the size of a pocketbook.

'How is it operated?'

'Quite simple. Here is the safety-catch. You push it down. Then, whenever you press this green button it starts the radio signal that activates the bomb.'

'Give it to me', Rao said.

'No', Paddy answered. 'I'll operate it.'

'May I not have a look?'

Paddy handed it to him. Rao looked attentively, then returned the instrument.

'I will tell you when to press it', Rao said. 'The most appropriate moment is the unveiling of the plaque by the District Collector and his declaring the canal open.'

'I have a problem', Jim stated. 'We agreed nobody should get hurt. People may flock to the dam at that moment to see the sluices open.'

'So what?'

'We should explode the bomb earlier.'

'When?'

'As soon as the District Collector begins to speak. I will take up position near the dam. I'll make sure no one is close enough to get hurt. Then I'll give Paddy a sign that he may go ahead.'

Rao objected but Jim and Paddy stuck to this arrangement. Suppressing annoyance at their opposition with ill grace, he gave in.

'All right. As long as it will be blown up.'

'What about the escape?'

'The Landrover will be ready. You'll find it parked on the road to the village, about a hundred yards away from the dam. If you pack your things now, I'll have them picked up and put into the Landrover beforehand.'

Jim went across to the school to meet Sundari. He realised he might not have an opportunity to say goodbye to her later so he wanted to speak to her a final time.

The school had lost its usual air of calm and discipline. Families were coming in and out. Classrooms had been converted into dressing rooms where girls were changing into the multi-coloured costumes used for dances. Jim understood that the school had shouldered the task of presenting the entertainment at the function.

Sundari was engaged in a last-minute rehearsal of a simple dance with some of the youngest children. Jim watched how she gave directions and occasionally stopped the group to demonstrate steps and movements herself. She had become so much a part of the people. They accepted her leadership with unconditional trust.

When she was satisfied, she spoke some words of encouragement, then dismissed the girls to get dressed in their special costumes.

'Hello', she said to Jim. 'Do you fancy a job on the stage?'

'No thank you.'

'What can I do for you?'

'Any further rumours?'

'No. But I'm still anxious. People expect something to happen. Some of the Madiga parents have withdrawn their

172

girls from the dance. There's fear in the air.'

'I see.'

'Have you come for a special purpose?' Sundari said again. 'I have a lot to do just now. After it's all over we'll have plenty of time. We could have a chat then.'

'I've got to leave the village today', Jim said. 'Because of the function we're staying as long as we can, but we'll be dashing off even before it's all finished. I didn't want to leave without saying goodbye to you.'

'That's kind.'

'I want you to know that I admire you. You're doing marvellous work.'

'Thank you. I'm sorry you're going because there was still a lot I wanted to say to you.'

'Such as?'

'Change your mind on violence. It has no place in a Christian attempt to heal conflict. Jesus overcame violence by love.'

'Wrong', Jim said. 'Jesus brought love through violence!'

'You can't mean that!'

'I do. The Father sent his Son to die on the cross. All right, his intention was to bring reconciliation. But it was brought about by Jesus' bloody, painful, violent death on the cross.'

'So you believe God wanted to see blood?'

'Yes. God's anger was only satisfied when he had seen the blood of his son.'

'My God!' Sundari exclaimed. 'You're still one of those antiquated blood worshippers. What you believe is neither Christian nor Catholic! Jesus did not die because God wanted to see blood.'

'No?'

'No. He died because some pharisees and other Jewish leaders opposed him. He foresaw that they wanted to kill him and he could have escaped. But he knew that he would then fall short in his leadership. As he says in the Gospel: 'I'm a shepherd who is concerned about my sheep. A hireling runs away when he sees a wolf coming. But I'm ready to give my life for the sheep'.'

'Then why did Jesus pray in Gethsemani: 'Father, let this cup pass me by; but not my will, but your will be done!'?'

'You see, it *was* the Father's will, but not the way you think it was!'

'How then?'

Sundari sighed, recalling the pressure of the moment. But she could not break off the argument half way. She continued with an edge of impatience in her voice.

'God did not want Jesus to die as if he himself demanded it. By becoming one of us, his Son redeemed the human race by every one of his actions whether big or small. He did not need to shed a drop of blood. If God's anger needed to be satisfied, surely redemption was no longer a question of forgiveness, of mercy, of a free gift to us. How can you call it a free gift if it had to be paid for in blood? Doesn't Scripture say that God *is* love, that there isn't in him a shade of darkness? How could you square that with a cruel, satisfaction demanding, Shylock type of a God?'

Jim was stunned. He had never considered it from that point of view. Sundari, sensing she was having an impact, continued.

'Yes, God wanted his Son to die, but not in an absolute sense, or for himself, to satisfy his anger, as I have explained. He wanted it only because he wanted his Son to be a good shepherd who would show his love for us by not deserting us in the hour of need, who would die out of love for us. Imagine a father whose son is an officer in the army. When there is a war, the father obviously doesn't want his son to get killed. But if the son leads his soldiers into battle, the father will not want his son to desert them. And this is what Jesus says: 'My Father loves me because I give my life freely for my sheep.' There is no violence in God.'

'That's quite a lecture', Jim said trying to recover his balance.

'I'm sorry we have so little time. Many Catholics and Protestants still have this old satisfaction idea in their heads. It's not scriptural. It's contrary to the teaching of great theologians like Thomas Aquinas. It's really the invention of legalists who project their own petty-mindedness on to God. But the consequences are horrendous. Many Christians have become hard and cruel because they believe God is hard and cruel.'

'You've given me a lot to think about.'

'Well, this is my last message to you. Get hold of a Bible and read St. John's first letter. He says it so clearly. God is love. We know God if we know love. We have no idea who God is, if we don't understand love. God is not present where there is hatred, injustice, violence.'

Jim was still reeling under the impact of Sundari's words. It was as if she had pricked a deep wound and pus was now flowing out. It brought release, and also pain. It filled him with a sense of elation, but also with bewilderment as if the pillars of his mental make-up had been shaken.

In a daze he left the school. He passed the majestic banyan tree in the middle of the village with the stone slabs on which the elders used to sit. He went over and sat down. In front of him was the statue of Prataparudra Deva, the young man who had given his life for the State of Andhra Pradesh. An old gentleman in white clothes removed a wreath of withered flowers and lovingly put a fresh one round the statue's neck. Jim realised it must be the youth's father, the village Brahmin.

Suddenly the similarity in the old man's devotion hit him. This was exactly as Sundari had said. The Father did not want his Son to die. But the Father wanted his Son to be faithful to his mission of love and that required being prepared to die. The consequences were enormous. God the Father was not a cruel God, a God who wanted to see blood. God was truly a God of love . . . .

Jim bent forward, resting his head on his arms. There was silence in him, almost shock. He knew that what had knocked him over was not just Sundari's words, but Sundari herself. She embodied God's love, in contrast to the hardness he had embodied himself. Then a prayer welled up in him, spontaneously.

'My God, I've been wrong. I know it now. Yes, I've had it in my bones, the awareness that you are love. It makes sense to me in an unspeakable way. How could I have allowed myself to become a man of violence? I a priest, like Jesus dedicated to bring peace and love?'

Images from his priestly experience stood before his mind, images of people who had needed him as a priest. There was Roisin, emaciated and thin, her cheeks pale and hollow through constant exhaustion. He had found her one day in bed, terrified at the prospect of her eighth childbirth. The house had been a shambles. The children were too young to cope and Colm her husband was a lorry driver: away or drunk. Jim had rolled up his sleeves, had cleaned and cooked and put the children to bed. He had called in day after day till Roisin could manage again. When he had heard Colm was back in town he had gone over to the pub and given him a dressing down in front of the lads. Roisin had thanked him when the new child was born; not with words but by calling the boy after him. Jim knew he had been God's love to that family.

He also remembered Bridget. Seventy years old. In church every single day. Wouldn't hurt a fly. Riddled with scruples. At least twice a week she would want to go to confession. 'I've had temptations', she would say, 'evil thoughts. I've cast a roving eye.' Jim had tried to be really patient with her, to keep reminding her that God was not a bully, that her scruples did not please him. 'But I'm sinful', she would keep saying. 'You don't believe me. I'm dirty inside . . . . ' He had scolded her. But he had never turned her away. Because he knew she was lonely and insecure and needed the affirmation he could give.

He recalled that time on Sunday when everything seemed to go wrong. He had been distracted during Mass. His sermon had fallen flat, or so it seemed to him. The congregation had looked even duller and less responsive than usual. But after the service Mike and Colleen had come over with the children. 'I felt so close to God', Colleen had said. 'I looked at your face during Mass and saw you were radiating Christ.' The unexpected compliment had moved Jim deeply. She was not given to flattery. She meant it. God was using him in a way he did not understand.

Nuala had told him so in unequivocal terms. As a young priest Jim had fallen in love with her. He had often visited the hospital where she was a nurse. She was a really beautiful person, in body and spirit. Jim's heart began to beat faster even now when thinking of her. When Jim had taken her out, one evening, Nuala had told him straight. 'I would marry you if you weren't a priest. Your priesthood is precious to me. Don't ruin it and me by going on at me. You gave up marriage to serve God. You've been generous. People need dedicated men like you. I don't want to take you away from the priesthood or from people.'

Jim had known that she was right. Afterwards, when the confusion had blown over, he had been very grateful to Nuala for helping him preserve his ideal. Being a priest wasn't easy. But the cost, the 'giving', made it all the more worthwhile.

Jim recalled Rosaleen and Kevin, how he had tried to help them. He had been prepared then to give his life, even though it had not worked out well in the end. The real cause of Rosaleen's and Kevin's death was not God's will to wreak bloodshed, but the awful deluge of violence and counter-violence unleashed by human hatred. God had been pleased with him, he knew, because he had genuinely tried to give them wellbeing and life.

Jim recognised that the essence of his priesthood lay in such 'giving', in 'caring' as Jesus had done, in being God's love to others by giving what no one else could give. 'God is love', Sundari had said. His courtship with violence had been more disastrous than his infatuation with Nuala could ever have been . . . .

He prayed, with words and without words, aware that much would need to be sorted out. He would have to adjust his ideas. He would need to obtain forgiveness and disentangle himself from the ILF . . . .

Then he remembered the actual moment and the impending explosion . . . . More than before the risks pressed themselves on his mind and repulsion about the act itself. Suddenly clarity dawned on him. He should not under any circumstances allow the explosion to go on. He must prevent it at all costs.

Of course, he could refuse to set off the detonator. Still the risk of someone getting hold of it . . . . There was one sure way of preventing the explosion: he could remove the aerial from the bomb . . . .

He rose with his mind made up. He looked at his watch: nine o'clock! The function was to start in an hour's time.

TWENTY EIGHT

When Jim approached the area near the dam, he could see that people were already flocking to the place. Festivity and excitement hung in the air. A group of musicians were playing joyful melodies on a motley of instruments: a clarinet, a flute, a cymbal, two trumpets and a drum. People who had put on their best clothes sorted themselves out by social status. The notables of the village and prominent guests were given seats in the shaded area before the stage. The caste people sat on mats behind them. The harijans, or outcastes, were sitting still more to the back and on the sides bordering the field.

Jim too was conducted to a chair under the *shamyâna*, to his relief next to Paddy and somewhat to one side. Rao and Kameswari sat four rows to the front.

'How's things?' Jim asked Paddy.

'OK. All's ready to go.'

'Remember to hang on to the detonator for dear life and wait for my signal.'

'I'd understood you the first time', Paddy said truculently. 'I'm not dumb.'

'OK. Well, you stay here so that I can find you. I'll wander across to the dam to see if all is well. Please, hold my seat for me.'

Jim sauntered off as if he was just looking around. People greeted him and let him pass. He was sorry to be so conspicuous as a foreigner. He realised hundreds of eyes would be upon him whatever he would do. How would he be able to remove the aerial without attracting undue attention?

His heart sank when he got close to the dam itself. Many people were standing around it, obviously discussing its merits.

Some children were playing on the dam itself, while others tried to cross to the other side by walking on the beam that spanned the sluices.

Even if he managed to get among them, how could he remove the antenna unobtrusively?

A jeep coming from the village stopped beside him. From the place next to the driver a voice called out to him.

'Mr. Ferguson?'

It was Madhura Reddy, the panchayati president.

Jim went over.

'What can I do for you?'

'How are you?'

'Quite well. Thank you.'

'After the opening there will be a dinner in my house. Many guests will come including the District Collector. I invite you and your son to join us.'

'Thank you', Jim said with some hesitation.

'You will surely come?'

'Yes.'

'Good.'

Madhura searched Jim's face with his shrewd, penetrating eyes.

'I want a distinguished visitor like yourself to remember this feast for the rest of your life.'

More and more people were coming from all directions. The crowd near the dam and on it thickened. Jim walked up and stood among them as if he was seeing the dam for the first time. A teenager, perhaps someone studying in a college and at home for the occasion, began to explain to Jim, in broken English, how the irrigation system worked. Jim grasped this opportunity to get even closer to the dam. Prompted by his questions, he and his eager guide were soon in the middle of the dam standing near the sluices.

However, the crowd had swollen even more and all of them were closely following every move of this inquisitive foreigner who showed such an interest in their dam. How can I ever get them to look away? Jim thought in despair. And what would happen if the bomb were to go off at a moment like this with two hundred people standing around?

The situation improved as soon as the District Collector arrived. People started clapping and shouting. The crowd around the dam moved away to witness the reception. Only a few stayed back including Jim's new found friend.

'You're not going to see?' the boy inquired.

'Sure, I will', Jim replied knowing that the moment for action had come.

He turned round clumsily and deliberately misplacing his foot slipped down the slope of the dam right to the spot where the explosives were hidden. While scrambling up, he groped with his hand under the bush searching for the antenna. He felt nothing.

Acting as if he lost his balance again, he rolled over and searched more thoroughly. The antenna was not there. It had been taken away and the hole carefully filled with new earth!

All this had only taken seconds. Jim was sure the bystanders interpreted his fall as a simple accident. As he climbed back up, they came to meet him, extended their hands to pull him up onto the dam and helped him beat the dust from his shirt and trousers.

Jim thanked them and made his way back to his seat under the shamyâna.

The function had begun. On the stage two young girls, dressed in red saris with gold embroidery, danced an elaborate welcome for the chief guest, the District Collector. He sat in the front row facing the stage next to Madhura Reddy.

In a low voice Jim explained to Paddy what he had found.

'You're sure? You looked in the right place?'

'Positive.'

'It doesn't make sense', Paddy said. 'It's all a joke. Unless . . . . '

'Unless what?'

'Unless someone is doing a Dungannon on us.'

'A Dungannon?'

'Don't you remember? The IRA had planted a bomb near

the police station. The Loyalists found out and shifted the charge to a local pub so the IRA was trapped into blowing up their own people.'

'My God! You may be right. Someone may have shifted the bomb .... ! Where to, I wonder?'

'Probably under the stage, right in front of the main guests', Paddy said.

It began to make sense to Jim. This whole tale of blowing up the dam had been a farce! The real target from the beginning had been Madhura himself and the District Collector! If the explosion were to go ahead, it would result in a massacre of indescribable proportions.

'Stay put!' he told Paddy.

Then almost trembling with suppressed fury and anxiety he moved forward to Rao's and Kameswari's seats. Rao had gone, but Kameswari was there. Jim gestured she should come.

Together they moved away from the crowd till they were on the road where they could talk.

'What have you done?' Jim almost shouted.

'What do you mean?'

'Why have you moved the bomb?'

'Moved the bomb?'

She seemed genuinely surprised.

In a few words Jim described what he had found. He could see that Kameswari too was shaken by the news.

'Who could have done that?' she stammered.

'Rao, of course', Jim replied.

'No', she said, shaking her head vigorously. 'Rao has strong feelings. He hates Madhura but he's not stupid. An explosion among the crowd would also kill many of his own people. No, it's not Rao. He really wanted to explode the dam. He doesn't want to kill Madhura. He wants to humiliate him.'

'But then, who could have done it?'

'Let me think. It must be Beela Hanumantha Rao. He knew about the bomb .... If the charge were to explode under the stage, it's the caste people, both Reddies and Kammas, who would get hurt .... '

'Yes', Jim said. He also remembered what Sundari had told him about the three feathers of the dead crow passed around in the Madiga quarter. Could Beela have planned the explosion as the start of a Naxalite uprising?

He shared his thoughts with Kameswari.

'You're right', she said. 'We must tell Rao.'

'Where is Rao?'

'He was called away just before you came by a man called Upakash .... My goodness, if I'm not mistaken, Upakash is one of Beela's men .... '

'What shall we do?'

'I don't know.'

'Let's go back to Paddy, get hold of the detonator and then stop the function. As long as we have the detonator not much can happen. We can tell people a bomb may have been planted, evacuate the area and search for it.'

When they re-entered the shamyâna they found Paddy was no longer in his seat. A discreet enquiry from a neighbour revealed that Paddy too had been called away.

Meanwhile a junior group of girls of Sundari's school had taken the stage and, to the intense amusement of the crowd, were dancing with tiny lights in both hands.

'Wait', Kameswari whispered to Jim. 'If Beela has the detonator, we must not act rashly. One false move and he'll blow up the bomb immediately. Let's find him and negotiate.'

'What's to stop him from pressing the button now?'

'The children.'

'The children?'

'Yes. The children. There are Madiga children among them too. Beela won't antagonise his own caste by risking their lives.'

'You're right', Jim said. 'But then I've another proposal. You go and find Beela. Negotiate with him, stall him. I'll talk to Sister Sundari to make sure the dances continue.'

TWENTY NINE

Jim walked along the edge of the crowd to the area behind the stage which was screened off from the public's view. It was jampacked with girls in dance attire, make-up people, teachers and their helpers. Smiling his greetings as he pressed his way through, Jim managed to get close to Sundari.

'You?!' she exclaimed.

'Sundari, you must help me', he whispered.

'Now? Can't you see the dances are going on?'

'It concerns the girls too. Their safety. I have reason to believe someone has placed a bomb under the stage.'

'What?!'

'Yes. A bomb. A mine. A load of explosives. Enough to kill half the crowd.'

'My God! Then let's have everyone out and away - now.'

'We can't. The person who controls the explosion might then react in panic. He would blow up the bomb before the people had understood what we were trying to tell them.'

'So what can we do?'

'The explosion is planned for when the speeches begin. At least that's what we think. As long as the children dance we'll be safe. Could you ensure that the dances go on for some time. Then I'll go under the stage and look for the bomb.'

Sundari's face looked grim. But she nodded. She went over to some teachers, called the next group of dancers together and conveyed her instructions.

'The next dance will begin just now', she said. 'They will do the whole sequence twice over. It will give us ten minutes. After that, I could bring up the juniors again.'

'Marvellous', Jim said.

He went over to the stage, pushed aside the tarpaulin with which it was covered and looked underneath. It was pitch dark. When his eyes began to adjust to the light, he saw what he was up against. Fruit boxes had been piled on top of each other and fastened in rows to make the foundation over which planks had been laid to form the stage proper.

'Please, keep the tarpaulin open', Jim whispered to Sundari. 'I need light.'

Without waiting for an answer he crept on all fours into the narrow space between two rows of boxes. The music stopped. The crowd applauded. Jim could hear the feet of the dancers leave the stage. His heart stopped. The interval was agonising. But soon the thuds of other feet could be heard on the planks overhead. A new melody started. The feet began to move rhythmically.

The further he crept into the passageway, the more Jim realised how difficult his task was. And dangerous. He re-called the lessons he had received about setting explosives and how to disconnect them. The fear was always that the charge itself had been booby-trapped.

Would Paddy have done a thing like that? Then he breathed with relief at the thought it could not have been booby-trapped. How else could it have been shifted by Beela's men?

He searched the space between two rows of boxes. There was very little light. He had to supplement his vision by sweep-ing through the space with his arms. It meant creeping forward two feet, searching, then creeping forward again. It was taking a lot of time. What if he did not find it in ten minutes?

He finished one passageway, squeezed himself sideways to another between rows of boxes and continued his search. The space here was even darker than it had been before.

Suddenly there was some light. He looked back. Someone

was creeping towards him holding a lighted candle. It was Sundari. The candle swayed from left to right as she made her way towards him, crawling on her knees and one hand while holding the candle in the other.

'Good God! Be careful!' Jim said. 'If these boxes catch fire, nothing can stop the explosion.'

Sundari grimaced in return.

'I've sent away as many people as I could on various pretexts. What does the bomb look like?'

'Three jerry cans tied together.'

'Where are they most likely to be?'

'Somewhere in front and in the middle. Thanks for helping me.'

By the candlelight they could work much faster. They checked two, three, four clearings between the boxes. The stuffy warm air and his mounting anxiety made Jim perspire all over his body. The music stopped. Applause from the crowd as before. Feet leaving the stage .... Jim looked at Sundari, worried.

'Still one dance to come. Laid on extra.'

'How much time?'

'Five minutes.'

The new dancers came on, their tiny feet pattering on the planks. There was an enthusiastic welcome by the crowd.

'Where can it be?' Jim groaned.

'Perhaps inside the boxes?' Sundari said.

'We could never check all of them .... '

'Is there an antenna?'

'My God, you're right!'

Suddenly Jim realised the antenna might provide a clue. Thinking that the tarpaulin might block the radio waves, Beela's men would have looked for a place where a hole had been left in the front of the stage .... Perhaps the place where the microphone leads had been installed ....

'Come', he said.

They crept to where Jim remembered having seen the microphone, at the front of the stage, off centre, slightly to the right. And there they found the jerry cans .... They had been tied against a pile of boxes with the aerial leading up, its point poking through the hole made for the microphone lead.

'Thank God!' Sundari whispered.

'Stay at a distance', Jim said. 'Don't let the flame get near.'

Sundari moved back. In her anxiety she bumped against a row of boxes, lost her balance and dropped the candle. She fell on it, smothering its flame. Both Jim and Sundari breathed heavily with the fright it had given them.

'Don't worry', Sundari whispered. 'I've got matches.'

Before Jim could say anything she had lit a match and rekindled the candle.

'Stay put!' Jim said.

The music had stopped. There was a thunderous applause. But Jim did not hear the noise. With total concentration, sweat pouring down his face, he gently put his hand on the place where the antenna entered the opening of one of the jerry cans. He pulled it up ever so carefully, then with his other hand felt how it had been connected. Then, shaking with tension he unwound the end of the aerial with his fingers. Then he pulled up the electrical fuse itself and threw it aside.

He sighed with intense relief.

Then leaning back to where Sundari lay crouched holding the candle, on impulse he kissed her on the cheek.

'We've done it!'

He tasted the salt of her tears on his lips. Over their heads on the stage a deep voice began to speak: Madhura Reddy!

'Let's get out of here!' Jim said. 'And be careful with that candle. We can do without a fire just now.'

While Sundari crept ahead, Jim followed, dragging the jerry cans with him as well as he could.

Dishevelled and covered in dust and dirt Sundari and Jim emerged from under the stage. They looked round: the teachers and children had left the off-stage area. Instead they saw an officer flanked by four policemen, holding guns. Colonel Pattabhi Rao was with them.

'Is he the man you mean?'

'Yes', he said.

I belong to State Security. I arrest you, both of you, for plotting an act of terrorism and inciting a riot. And what's in those cans?'

'You'll find them full of explosives', Rao said.

'I can explain everything', Sundari stated.

'I hope so, for your sake'.

THIRTY

They were taken by jeep to the police station in the village. Jim demanded to see the officer immediately. He was given no more than five minutes.

Seated in the small office of the local constable behind a rickety wooden table obviously below his status, the officer dismissed Jim's account.

'You have been hired by Naxalites to start a riot. Harijan informers alerted us to what was to come. The explosion you were to set was the signal for a wholesale revolt.'

'It was Colonel Pattabhi Rao who planned the explosion.'

'I don't believe you. The Colonel works for State Security and through him we arrested you just in time. Anyway, I won't argue with you. You can explain yourself in court.'

Jim and Sundari were locked up in a bare detention room with no more than a few mats along the wall.

'I can't believe it', Jim said as they sat down. 'Surely the man could see we were removing the explosives, not placing them.'

'There's more behind it', Sundari agreed. 'Why don't you tell me whatever you know. Don't you think I'm entitled to it?'

'You are', Jim said. 'But if I tell you the whole story you'd be shocked. You'd reject me for ever.'

'I promise you, I won't. I've seen you risk your life to dismantle the bomb.'

'Thank you.'

The need of telling everything, of sharing all he had done, welled up in him. If anyone might help him, it would be Sundari. He might shock her .... Then again, she had proved to be tough and able to face real situations.

'It will be like a general confession .... '

And, slowly at first, then more rapidly, he began to speak.

'Paddy is not my son', he said, 'but a colleague.' Then he revealed to her that he was a priest and that he had become involved in the nationalist cause. He shared his anger, his hopes and anxieties; the despair and suffering he had seen among Catholics and how he had decided to join them in their struggle. Finally, omitting the names of people and places, he recounted his part in the killing of a British official, his journey to India and what had happened in the final weeks.

Sundari had become as white as a sheet. She closed her eyes at times, then looked at him as if to give him encouragement.

'I know I've made a mess of things', Jim concluded. 'But then God knows, I've tried to do what was best. Your sermon this morning on God being love and God not wanting violence, not even in the case of Jesus' death, touched me deeply. What can I do to pick up the pieces? If I'm hauled before an Indian court, the whole thing will come out. Moreover, will I ever be worthy to say Mass again, with blood on my hands?'

Sundari put her hand on his own.

'Thank you for trusting me. What we need to do is to pray. You need healing and forgiveness. I need inner strength to help you and to forgive.'

They prayed in silence.

Sundari began to speak again.

'My mother was a Hindu, a very saintly person. Like Gandhi she believed in *ahimsa*, non-violence. I have seen her suffer incredible hardships with great patience. 'We must always forgive', she used to tell me. I learned from her how love defeats hatred and tolerance bigotry. Her gentleness was strong. I wish she could be here now to give me advice . . . . But then, I know what she would say . . . . '

Sundari buried her face in her hands. Jim watched her anxiously. Now there were no secrets between them. They had reached a new level of intimacy. But he had also erected new barriers . . . .

An hour later one of the guards brought in a tray of food. He put it on the floor in front of them and left. There was a glass of water for each and a tin plate filled with rice and *dhal*.

Under one of the plates they found a folded piece of paper. It turned out to be a letter from Paddy.

'Rao has done the dirty on us', it said. 'Neither I nor Kameswari know what he is up to. Don't worry. Kames has friends. We're working on a plan to free you.'

It was reassuring to know that Paddy was still at large and that Kameswari was on their side. What about Rao? Jim too found it difficult to understand why Rao wanted to have him arrested. Could it not lead to some of his own shady activities getting exposed? Surely it was not a risk Rao would want to take.

They ate their food in silence.

It looked as if they had been deserted. Apart from two policemen guarding the station, no one else was around. Music wafted in from the far distance.

'They're all at the celebrations', Sundari observed.

They had not spoken for some time. Sundari was absent-minded and withdrawn, Jim noticed. His story had affected her more than she would let on. She was still adjusting to the shock of finding out that he was a priest, and had been involved in murder.

'This security man who got killed, what kind of man was he?' she asked all of a sudden.

'Why?'

'Did you know him?'

'A little.'

'Tell me about him.'

Jim drew a deep breath.

'You're right, I suppose. I should have thought of him as

another human being. Perhaps I did, to some extent. He wasn't a bad sort. He was the kind of man who was chosen for a top job because he was tough. But he was also fair. On a number of occasions he instigated proceedings against prison wardens who had ill-treated prisoners. He wanted them punished not only for appearance's sake. He believed in justice. I also know for a fact that he was ready to compromise on the issue of the hunger strike. He was a man I would be able to respect. But, of course, in my eyes he was the enemy.'

Sundari closed her eyes and remained silent for some time. Then she raised her head and looked Jim straight in the eyes.

'If you were to meet him today, would you still kill him?'

'Are you trying to find out if I'm still a murderer at heart?'

'Answer me, as honestly as you can.'

'If I still had the frame of mind I was in at the time, I probably would . . . . Remember also, I got drawn in. I did not foresee he would get killed. But given my attitude at the time, I would probably allow it to happen; as I did. But now, I'm not sure. You've really changed my thinking and I agree with you it was probably a big mistake. I'm still confused about it though. Let me put it like this: the way I'm feeling now, I'm having second thoughts about the use of violence. I'm sure you're right in saying violence is not really a Christian response.'

Sundari still held his eyes.

'You're evading my question. Can't you be more decisive than that? Would you, or would you not, take part in his killing?'

'You hang on like a terrier', Jim said. 'I suppose I wouldn't.'

'Make up you mind whether you're a soldier or a priest.'

'Remember, that may not be an either - or. Gaelic blood runs through my veins. Among the Celts even priests are warriors.'

'It's time you got converted', she answered. 'You're a Christian, are you not?'

'I'll tell you a story', Jim said.

'Do', Sundari replied.

'In county Antrim, in the small village of Neldincum, farmers used to organise an annual event which they called 'riding the bull'.

'In the afternoon of Ascension day they'd gather in a meadow. They'd set up a low circular fence in the middle to make some kind of arena. In it a one year old bull would be released. On purpose the bull had been kept in the dark for a week so that it would be really wild when it came out into the light. It would run around in the ring and be quite a fearsome sight to behold.

'The young men would then begin to challenge each other to ride the bull. Some would lay wagers and go for the money. But for the most part it was a question of honour. I don't know how to describe what exactly went on in people's minds. It was frightening and exhilarating at the same time. Let me put it this way: if a young farmer was seriously being challenged to ride the bull and he chickened out, it would affect his standing in the community for good. Even the women would despise him and call him a coward. Once you were challenged, you had no choice. You *had* to go, whether you liked it or not. Almost every year someone would get hurt.

'The aim was to stay on top of the bull for at least one full minute. But even if you were thrown off, your honour was saved, as long as you'd somehow managed to get onto its back.

'Now I was appointed to that village as chaplain. I'd heard about the event and decided to go along, to see it for myself. It was foolish of me to go, I suppose. The clergy had always stayed away. But I thought I must be where my people are.

'They were surprised to see me turn up, but it didn't stop them from playing their game. A strong hefty bloke wrestled with the bull, was thrown off, scrambled to safety across the fence and was applauded as a hero. Then they challenged Leonard, a thin individual, a new farmhand who'd come in from another part of the county. He drew back, fear showing on his face. They heckled him. I could see the man tremble.

'Leave him alone!' I said.

'All turned round to look at me. From being an observer, I'd become an intruder.

'A cheeky young lad shouted, 'You go, Father!'

'Yes, yes!' others joined in. '*You* ride the bull. Father O'Brien, show what stuff you're made of!'

'All looked at me with a mixture of expectation and derision. They knew quite well that I was a city man, born in Belfast, with no experience of handling cattle.

'I was in a fix and my blood began to boil. But I decided to stay cool. I wasn't going to let myself be goaded into doing what I couldn't do. So I bit my lip and kept quiet.

'Leonard climbed over the fence. His face was pale and his hands trembled, but he knew he could not escape the ordeal. He tried to sneak up behind the bull but he was too slow. The bull whipped round and butted its forehead against Leonard's chest. He fell backwards and lay flat on the ground, the bull standing over him. Everyone yelled.

'At that moment I'd had enough. I pushed people aside, jumped the fence and kicked the bull against its flank, to draw it away from Leonard. The bull turned to me. Its nostrils flared with rage. Its hoofs scraped the ground. Its blood-shot eyes looked straight at me.

'Suddenly the fear I'd felt subsided. A deep confidence took hold of me, the kind of confidence St. Francis of Assisi must have felt when he confronted the wolf.

'I fixed my eyes on the bull. 'Steady, old boy', I said. '*You're* not at fault. It's these stupid lads.'

'I took another two steps forward, transfixing the bull with my eyes. I could see the expression on its face change from anger to a plea for help.

'Again I stepped forward till I could grasp its horns with my two hands. Gently, ever so gently, I pressed its head down. It snorted, but surrendered. It bent its knees and lay before me meek as a lamb.'

Sundari looked at Jim.

'Did it really happen?'

'No', he said. 'It's something I dreamed, long ago.'

At half past two their peace was shattered. Quite unexpectedly the sound of a huge explosion rent the air. Jim and Sundari jumped up, dazed by the blast. The original thunder of the main explosion was followed by the rumble of some minor explosions, then a deadly calm.

'My God!' Jim exclaimed. 'What has happened?'

A few minutes later they could hear a wave of new noises: shouting and crying, the rat-a-tat of gunfire, the shrieking of children running through the streets in panic.

'This must be the trouble people were expecting', Sundari said. 'The riot.'

'What can we do?'

'Let's call the guards.'

They banged on the door. No response.

'The police must have gone to have a look', Jim said. 'Let's try to get out.'

He examined the ramshackle wooden door of the detention room. It did not appear too much of an obstacle. He stepped back, then lurched forward, throwing his whole weight against it. It gave way, partly. He repeated the exercise and this time the lock broke.

A few seconds later they stood outside. People were running to and fro in the narrow streets of the village. In the background they could still hear the noise of fighting and shouting. Sundari stopped an elderly woman and asked what had happened. The answer was a cascade of tearful sentences.

'As far as I can make out, a bomb went off at Madhura's party. Some prominent people were killed. Then fighting erupted. Some armed bands of Naxalites are attacking the houses of Reddies and Kammas, murdering families and looting. No one knows where it will stop.'

'Where shall we go?'
'I must go to the hostel to see if my children are safe.'
They ran through the streets on the way to the convent.

THIRTY ONE

Avoiding the centre of the village where most of the fighting seemed to go on, Sundari and Jim reached the mission compound.

The other Sisters were delighted to see Sundari back. So were the boarding children. They hugged her and danced around her, forgetting for a moment the turmoil going on outside.

At that very moment a Landrover turned into the gates of the compound. The driver hooted to make a way through the children. The car stopped and a middle-aged European Sister came out.

'Monica!' Sundari exclaimed, stepping forward to welcome her. 'What a day to come on a visit!'

'Indeed. The whole village is in uproar. Like an ants' nest that has been stirred. What's going on?'

'Fighting!'

'Oh, my God!'

Sundari turned to Jim.

'Meet my friend, Sister Monica. Classmate, colleague, and now my boss as assistant provincial. Of the finest Irish vintage.' Introducing Jim she said: 'Jim Ferguson is from Northern Ireland. He's here on a short holiday. We've already become close friends in just a couple of days.'

After an exchange of greetings, Sundari inquired: 'Why have you come? There must be an urgent reason .... since you didn't write!'

'There is. I'll tell you all about it. But let me first settle in and have a bath.'

'Of course.'

Sundari arranged for Monica's luggage to be taken from

the Landrover and carried into the Sisters' convent.

'You and the girls seem to be all right just now', Jim told her. 'I must go and find Paddy.'

'Where will you look for him?'

'At Kameswari's place.'

'All right. But be careful. Remember Colonel Rao . . . . '

Jim was already on his way back.

Running as fast as he could, he ignored the warnings of people who were fleeing from the Kamma quarter and reached the Yeddanapudi home in ten minutes' time. The street was deserted but when he entered the compound he saw a number of men gathered on the main verandah.

They were five swarthy men carrying long knives and scythes standing round a person who lay on the floor. Jim came closer, saw a sari and realised it must be Velamma. The men looked round. They had obviously been kicking and beating the old woman.

Jim guessed they wanted something from her. The key to the strong box perhaps. Or information on Kameswari's whereabouts. After obtaining what they wanted, they would probably finish her off . . . .

Lack of courage had never been his problem. He leapt on to the verandah, picked up a steel chair and brandishing it about, charged in on the men. They shrank back at first, then re-grouped, trying to encircle him and swiping at him with their knives.

Jim knew he was outnumbered. He would not be able to keep up this unequal fight for long. Once or twice the knives had come dangerously close to his arms.

Suddenly a penetrating, loud wail began somewhere else in the village. It was a new sound, as if thousands of voices at once were raised in sorrow and protest.

The men stopped. One of them ran into the street to look. He came back shouting and pointing at the sky. Then of one accord all turned and ran out of the compound.

Infinitely relieved Jim too went into the street and looked.

A large, black column of smoke rose from the side of the

village the wailing came from . . . .   He realised it was the
Madiga quarter. It must have caught fire . . . .

Jim went back. He picked up Velamma who had been badly
bruised and who was only half conscious. He carried her inside
and laid her on her bed. She recognised him and murmured
'Thank you'.

Jim told her, as well as he could, to close and lock the door
after his departure.

Then he ran back to the mission compound which adjoined
the Madiga quarter.

On the way he witnessed horrendous scenes. The bamboo
and reed huts in street after street were blazing with fire. In
utter panic people were trying to save their property, or to save
the elderly and children who might have stayed behind in the
house. There was weeping and crying. On many faces he saw
despair as one finds only among those who have lost everything.

Jim tried to help. He saw a man entering a smouldering hut.
He gathered someone might have been left behind. The hut's
roof had already partly collapsed. With the man Jim entered
the black smoke and searched the glowing debris with his shoes
and with a piece of wood he held in his hand. Under the ashes
on the floor he felt a soft bundle. He dug it out and lifted it.
Almost choking, he carried it outside on his arms. Then he saw:
he was holding the charred body of a child! The mother cried
out in anguish as she took it from his hands.

Many people had been wounded and were being carried to
the clinic in the mission compound. Jim joined them holding on
his shoulders a ten-year old boy whose left leg was burnt from
ankle to thigh.

The little church had gone up in flames. The other mission
buildings, both convent and hostel, had mercifully escaped.

People thronged the compound. Rows of sick and dying lay
stretched out on the ground. surrounded by sorrowing relatives. The Sisters were moving from case to case, helping as
well as they could. Bandages had run out, so Sundari had
ordered that all available sheets be cut in strips and used in-

stead. In most cases little more could be done than provide primitive first aid and human comfort.

'Here are some Catholics who are dying', Sundari told Jim. 'Give them absolution. Pray for them. Help them. You're a priest!'

'What about the Holy Oils?'

'Burnt with the church'.

Jim went round, prayed, imposed hands. Never in his life had he felt so inadequate, not speaking the language, not being able to give any real help. Yet he moved from one person to the other, tears in his eyes at the suffering he witnessed, praying for them all with his heart. And, he could see, people responded.

An angry mob surged from the street into the compound. They were armed with clubs and sticks and shouted demands. Sundari tried to stop them. They talked to her. She answered back. Holding the mob in control through her sheer personality, she sent one of the Sisters to Jim.

'Sister Sundari tells you to run to the convent and lock yourself in. These men have come to beat you up. She says:'Remember the three feathers'.'

Jim did as he was told. He ran to the convent, closed the doors and locked them from the inside. He heard a howl outside. Angry men surrounded the small building on all sides, and began pounding on its doors and windows with fists and sticks.

Inside the convent Jim went round the various rooms on the ground floor to make sure all windows had been secured. They were. He drifted into the small, half-lit room the Sisters used as their chapel. He saw the red flame of the sanctuary lamp which told him where the Blessed Sacrament was being preserved.

On impulse he knelt down before it on both knees.

Turmoil outside. People who wanted to beat him up. Turmoil in his own country where he was wanted for murder.

Turmoil in his mind and in his heart. Would he ever have peace again?

He turned his face towards the tabernacle and watched the ever changing pattern of light and shadow thrown against the walls by the flickering flame.

Would God understand?

Would God accept him again as a priest, in spite of the horrible mess he had made of his life?

Sundari had said God would.

Jim buried his face in his hands and felt an enormous longing for cleansing, healing, reconciliation. It sprung from deep inside him and inundated his whole being as a flood of turbulent emotion. He felt it as an unspoken prayer, a plea to God for which he could not find the words . . . .

Unexpectedly he felt a tap on his shoulder. He turned round. It was Sister Monica.

'Sorry to disturb your prayer. I need your advice.'

'Of course', Jim said, getting up and trying to regain his emotional balance.

'Can we go to the parlour?'

THIRTY TWO

'I have upsetting news for Sundari', Monica began. 'I don't know how to break it to her. When I found you praying in the chapel and knowing you're her friend .... '

'I'm not sure', Jim said.

'You see, Sundari and I have known each other for a long time. I always seem to rub her the wrong way, whether I want it or not. It's difficult to explain. Perhaps, she'll take it better from you ....   Moreover, she too is from Northern Ireland in a manner of speaking.'

'Is she?'

'Yes. Didn't she tell you? Her mother was Indian, but her father was British. From Northern Ireland, to be precise.'

Jim was stunned. Suddenly Sundari's emotional responses concerning the Ulster troubles began to make sense to him.

'What is the bad news?' Jim stammered.

'Her father has been killed, some five weeks ago. Through poor communications I only found out two days back. You see, the family have never really accepted Sundari. They never approved of her becoming a Catholic, then a nun and on top of that we're an Indian congregation ....   It will be a terrible blow to her.'

'I thought her father died ages ago. She said she lost him when she was young.'

'She lost him - yes; but not through death. He deserted his wife and his child.'

'Who was her father?' Jim asked, sudden fear choking his voice.

'Peter Bowyer, governor of Lough Mann detention centre.'

Jim froze. The enormity of this unexpected connection with Sundari overwhelmed him. He had killed her father! How awful! What a coincidence that he was to meet Sundari of all people in the world. Or was it a coincidence? Associations and emotions flooded his mind. Eventually he spoke.

'But she never talked about her links with Northern Ireland.'

'I'm not surprised. She had a harrassing youth in Belfast.'

'Tell me.'

'Peter Bowyer served in the military police at Poona barracks immediately after the war. He fell in love with Tripura Krishnamoorthy, a Brahmin lady who worked in administration as a clerk. They got married and Sundari was their only child.

'As long as they remained in India, things were all right. When Peter was transferred to Belfast, he took Tripura and Sundari with him. Then difficulties started. Peter was a strict Protestant and his family rejected his marriage. People in Northern Ireland are not as used to mixed marriages as people in England. To have an Indian wife and a dark-skinned child was an embarrassment to Peter. So he moved his family to Dublin and gave them a pension on condition they would stay away. Sundari has always felt that she was disowned by her father.

'Her mother died when she was in college. As a young teacher, she fell in love with a Catholic and decided to become a Catholic herself; first for his sake, then out of conviction. The boy's family wrecked the relationship.

'While making a long journey to India, she discovered her religious vocation. She realised that India is her real mother-country and she joined our congregation. She's highly respected by all because she's so dedicated in her work.

'The one thing Sundari never sorted out is her relationship to her father. I know that she always wanted to go and see him and be reconciled. His sudden death has made that impossible. She'll be very much upset, I know, and that's why I don't know how to tell her. If it comes from me, it will be like making her feel a failure once more.'

Jim sat back, closed his eyes and thought. *My God, what are you doing to me? Why did you make me meet Sundari after killing*

*her father? Are you rubbing in how stupid I've been? How can I
ever face her again?'*

He suddenly remembered Peter Bowyer's last request. 'Tell
my daughter Evelyn that I'm sorry . . . . ' 'Sister', he said.
'Did Sundari have another name before she joined?'

'Yes, Evelyn. She took 'Sundari Frances' as her religious
name when she made her profession. Why do you ask?'

'Never mind. Please,give me time to think.'

Both sat in silence. The noise outside was subsiding a little.
The banging on the walls and windows had stopped. There was
still the noise of the crowd in the compound.

Someone rattled the front door. It was Sundari.

'You can open up', she shouted. 'The men have disappeared. You're safe. I need to get in.'

'Will you tell her, please?', Monica asked.

Jim swallowed. He would have to face her anyway.

'I will', he promised. 'Not just now. At the right time.'

The hostel, the school building , the clinic were full of sick
and wounded, Sundari reported. Some of the worst cases
would need to be put up in the Sisters' bedrooms.

A number of emergencies had already been dispatched to
the hospital in Doodgaon in whatever cars were available. It
would be long night of nursing the sick till ambulances from the
hospital and another caravan of cars could pick up the remaining casualties.

'It's been a terrible day for Yuddhapalli', Sundari said. 'The
fire has killed at least a hundred people in the Madiga quarter.
About twenty Reddies and Kammas died on account of the
blast and the subsequent fighting. No one knows exactly what
took place. Madhura and the District Collector survived.
Madhura's wife and daughter are among the victims. He's a
broken man. We're expecting the army to come in from Adila-

bad to put the village under military control.'

'It's time for me to get out', Jim thought.

He remembered the accusation made by the police. He would certainly be held for interrogation, if not be made a convenient scapegoat. On the other hand, he needed to talk to Sundari. He could not possibly leave the village without telling her everything and making peace with her. Also he was responsible for Paddy. He needed to locate him urgently.

'Sundari', Jim said. 'Since calm has returned to the village, let me go once more to see if I can find Paddy.'

'Alright. But don't walk through the Madiga quarter.'

'I won't.'

'Will I see you again?'

Jim looked into her eyes.

'Yes', he said. 'In an hour's time I'll be back. Please wait for me. There's something more I need to tell you.'

'OK. Look after yourself.'

In the Yeddanapudi home Jim found Paddy and Kameswari.

'Where have you been?', Paddy exclaimed.

Kameswari came up to him, fell at his feet and hugged him by the knees.

'You've saved my mother's life', she said. 'Thank you a thousand times. I will always be indebted to you.'

She took Jim into her mother's room. Velamma was lying on bed, weak but smiling.

'My mother told me everything', Kameswari said again. 'The men were after me and Rao. They would have killed her if it hadn't been for your timely intervention.'

Jim accepted their thanks protesting it had only been his duty.

'I missed Paddy', he said. 'Together we would have made short work of them.'

'We would!', Paddy said grimly. Jim had risen sky high in

his esteem through this bout of valour.

Back on the verandah, Jim demanded an explanation.

'Where have you been the whole day?'

'Remember you went to look at the dam?', Paddy said. 'I was called out by a man who said he had a message from Rao. I believed him. He took me some distance down the road towards the village. Then I found myself surrounded by three men, hefty blokes all of them, and I realised they were after the detonator. You'd told me not to let it out of my hands so I weighed into them before they could think. Two of them I laid out flat and the third ran away. I tried to go back but saw more men coming my way, so I ran into the village and, making a detour, decided to come back here and lock myself into my room. I reckoned you'd figure that out sooner or later.'

'Well done!' Jim said.

'After we parted I met Beela Hanumantha Rao', Kameswari continued the story. 'He was furious. From the way he demanded the detonator, I realised Paddy had got out of his clutches. So to stall time I promised to look for Paddy and get it from him. He didn't trust me, however. I heard him give instructions to set fire to the stage. That too would have exploded the bomb.'

'It would', Jim agreed. Then he recounted how he and Sundari had found the bomb and made it safe.

'What I don't understand', he said, 'is Rao's complicity in having us arrested by the police'.

'Rao is a genius', Kameswari said. 'He works for the police as an informer which, in reality, means he can use the police as he sees fit. Rao knew what you were doing. By that time the place was teeming with Beela's men. The only way of getting you and those explosives out safely was to have you arrested temporarily.'

'Hmm. That sounds plausible', Jim said.

'You see, Beela double-crossed Rao. Instead of just attacking the Reddies, he wanted a riot that would eliminate all the leaders, both Reddy and Kamma. Blowing up the stage was just a start to get the riot going. When that failed Beela managed to get the explosives all the same and he had them taken into Madhura's compound on a rickshaw. It only needed a burning torch for the whole house to be blown up.'

'Where were the two of you all the time?'

'Rao told us to go to a little pump house two miles outside the village. It belongs to a relative of ours and is a convenient place of refuge. I never expected they would molest my mother, otherwise I would have taken her as well.'

'And what about the fire in the Madiga quarter?'

'That was another of Rao's brilliant ideas. You see, Rao too was among the guests at Madhura's party. Fortunately he escaped. He stood near the gate, not near the house.

When he saw the blast and the fighting that erupted, he grasped Beela's real purpose: to kill off the leading caste families. Beela relied mainly on support from the Madigas. The only way to stop the Madigas was to burn their houses. It was brilliant. It saved the village.'

'It was terrible', Jim countered. 'Do you know that about a hundred people were burnt to death? And then the casualties. Some will be maimed and handicapped for life.'

'It's unavoidable in war', Kameswari observed.

Jim fell silent. It was the kind of thing he might have said two months ago.

'We have to move', he then said briskly. 'The army is moving in, to seal off the village and restore order. We must get out before they block our escape.'

'Right. The car is ready. We've put in your luggage and provisions. We are going to the pump house and my mother is coming along.'

'OK. But on the way we need to stop at the mission compound. There's one thing that remains to be done.'

THIRTY THREE

Kameswari, Velamma and Paddy stayed in the car outside the mission compound while Jim got out.

'Make it short!', Kameswari urged. Little did she realise the ordeal Jim had to face.

He hurried to the convent. Sundari was not there. She was probably in the hostel, he was told, nursing the sick. He ran across and found her moving down the corridor from one make-shift mattress to the next.

'Sundari', Jim said with great urgency in his voice. 'Can we go somewhere where we can be alone? I have to talk to you and time is running out.'

'Are the police after you?'

'They may be.'

'You want me to hide you?'

'No! Please, it's something else. Where can we go?'

Sundari thought.

'On the roof of the building.'

Via a narrow, concrete stairway they reached the flat roof of the hostel. The three-quarter moon gave little light behind thick clouds. It was quite dark.

Jim fell on his knees before Sundari and began to cry. His body shook with his uncontrollable sobbing. It was an utter breakdown of all his pride and self control.

Sundari was taken aback.

'Come on, come on!', she said. 'Calm down. Don't let yourself go like that!'

She put her arms around his shoulders and hugged him.

'Calm down. You're not a child. What's the matter? How can I help you?'

Jim forced himself to speak.

'Sundari', he whispered. 'Did you mean it when you said you believe God is love and always ready to forgive?'

'Of course', she said.

'Would you forgive me? Whatever I have done?'

'I would', she said again, firmly. 'Besides, you haven't hurt me in any way.'

'I have', Jim said, clutching her hands. 'Sundari, I've done the worse thing I could have done to you. The man I killed, I found out only this evening, that man was your father, the prison governor, Peter Bowyer.'

Sundari held Jim in silence. Her body had gone rigid.

'Was it my father?' she said. 'My father . . . . He never owned up to me as a child. I loved him you know. I wanted to be his friend, to be close to him. He never let me. It's the great sorrow of my life. And now he's dead . . . . '

'I'm so sorry', Jim said. 'I'm sorry having been involved at all. I'm all the more sorry since he was your father. Can you forgive me?'

'Come here', Sundari said. 'Get up. We can sit here on the parapet. I want to tell you a few things.

First of all, I have already forgiven you. When you told me your story this afternoon, I asked myself the question: 'Would I forgive him, if the victim had been my father?' I forgive you because I saw you were sorry and I wanted God to forgive you. How could I pray to God for your forgiveness, if I were not to forgive you?

Secondly, the greatest joy you can give me is to sort this whole business out in confession, to make up in any way you can and then forget about this part of your life. I want you to be a priest again, a man of God, someone who knows violence doesn't work and that God is love.'

'If only I can . . . . '.

'Of course you can. You will. What I regret most is that I haven't made peace with my father. Now it's too late. I intended to travel to Belfast some time and meet him face to face. I should have done so earlier. That's where I have failed to be God's love to him.'

'You have not', Jim said.

'I have', Sundari replied.

'No. You see, your father knew you loved him and he wanted to make up with you. I didn't tell you so this afternoon but before your father died he said to me: 'Tell my daughter Evelyn that I'm sorry. I've treated her badly. Tell her I'm sorry'.'

Now it was Sundari's turn to sob.

'Oh, Jim', she said, embracing him. 'I can't tell you how happy I am about that last message of his. It shows that he did love me. Now it's easy to forgive him with all my heart.'

'Yes', Jim said. 'I'm sure he did love you. You're the only one he was concerned about.'

'Jim', Sundari said suddenly. 'Is this why you came to Yuddhapalli? To give me my father's message?'

'Perhaps, yes. Not in my intention, but in God's plan I'm sure . . . . He wanted me to find you, so as to be converted and get forgiven . . . . '

'And to take me the message of my father's forgiveness.'

'When I became a Sister', Sundari continued, 'I no longer wanted to bear the name my father had given me. I chose the name 'Sundari Frances' because my mother called me 'Sundari' 'beautiful one' as my pet name and St Francis was disowned by his father and sent away naked. From today I will resume my true name. I will be called 'Sundari Evelyn' to honour my father and express our reconciliation.'

A dark figure appeared from the stairwell. It was Paddy.

'For Chrissake', he said. 'Three lorries full of soldiers have arrived in the village. They'll massacre us . . . . '

'I'm coming', Jim grunted in reply.

Jim and Sundari embraced each other.

'Evelyn', Jim said. 'I shall never forget you.

When Jim stood outside a few minutes later, he found

Kameswari waiting for him. She was alone. The vehicle was nowhere to be seen.

'Soldiers came round the corner', she said. 'I asked Paddy to go ahead with my mother. They got away just in time.'

'What about us?'

'We'll have to walk.'

'That's fine with me. Thank you for waiting for me.'

'I owe it to you. You rescued my mother.'

They walked in the shadows of a street that led out of the village. Kameswari stopped. A hundred yards ahead soldiers had thrown up a crude roadblock. Obviously the village was being sealed off.

'What next?' Jim asked as they took cover in the dark shadows of a hedge.

'The same will apply to all exits from the village.'

'So what?'

'We'll *have* to get out. Tomorrow all houses will be searched, you can be sure. Somehow or other we'll have to get past those guards.'

'What about the fields? Can't we do a cross country run?'

'They must have posted people there too. Anyway, we can have a try.'

'They moved cautiously along the hedge which had been fortified with bamboo sticks and thorn branches. They walked along till they reached a low gate. They climbed it and found themselves in a mango grove. Carefully picking their way in the dark, they crossed to the other side, moving as far away from the road as they could. Kameswari sought and found a hole in the hedge.

They crept through and landed in a field of half grown tobacco plants. These offered them little cover. To make matters worse, the clouds parted and the moon's silvery light was strong enough to give a wide view. If they tried to cross the field, the guards would certainly spot them. And they did not know if others had been posted further down along the far side of the field.

Lying on the ground between the tobacco plants, they

reviewed the options open to them, in hushed voices. By now their eyes had grown accustomed to the dark. There were two soldiers, they saw, one sitting on a piece of rock, the other pacing up and down, rifle slung from his left shoulder.

'Can't we overpower them?' Kameswari suggested.

'No chance', Jim said firmly. 'Moreover, I've seen enough violence for a long time to come. Count me out.'

'Perhaps they'll go to sleep', Kameswari said. 'Travelling in a lorry is no joke. They must be tired. Let's wait a little and see what happens.'

They lay there in silence, keeping their eyes on the two soldiers and listening to the sounds of the night. An old man came trudging down the road. The soldiers stopped him. He swore at them, then returned to the village.

Again silence.

What strange situations I've been in today, Jim mused. *And now I'm here in the middle of the night. Who'd have thought I'd land up in a tobacco field with an Indian woman at my side, trying to outwit soldiers who might blow off my head.*

Kameswari was thinking too.

'Jim', she whispered.

'Yes?'

'May I ask you a question?'

'Sure.'

'You know Paddy well, don't you?'

'Yes. Sort of.'

'Is he married?'

'No. He's single. Didn't he tell you?'

'He did.'

'Then why ask me?'

'Well, you know . . . .   men in a foreign country . . . .'

'He's not married.'

They were silent again.

'Do you think he'd be a good husband?' she asked again.

He looked at her. The expression on her face was serious. Her features shone in the light of the moon, fragile like ceramic. Should he tell her what he really thought?

212

'Did he propose to you?'

'He did.'

'Paddy's got a good heart . . . . but . . . . '

'But what?'

'Don't you think there's a risk it won't work out? There are vast cultural differences between the two of you.'

'But I *love* Paddy. And basically, human beings are the same anywhere in the world.'

'Would you come and live in Ireland?'

'I would.'

'You'd die of cold and misery . . . . You'd miss your sunshine and your chilies!'

'Yes . . . . but then, Paddy could live with me in Hyderabad, you know.'

'Would he like to?'

'I'm sure he would.'

They fell silent again. Jim felt strangely compassionate towards Kameswari and Paddy. Perhaps it *would* work out. They were two young people who had fallen in love . . . . But then he thought again of the incompatibilities between them.

'The question you must ask yourself', he formulated carefully, 'is this: Will Paddy make a good father to your children?'

'I don't need to ask that question.'

'No?'

'No.'

'Why not?'

She hesitated.

'He's already father to my child1'

'What? You're pregnant?'

'I am.'

'My God . . . . !'

'I haven't told him yet. I only found out yesterday myself. I don't know if it will change his feelings towards me.'

'Of course, it won't!' Jim said with a sudden surge of warmth. 'I'm sure he will be proud of you and of his child.' Then he held his breath as he remembered Peter Bowyer and his daughter Evelyn . . . .

Their attention was distracted by the soldiers. They spoke to each other. One detached himself and came slowly walking down the road. He turned and stepped into the field, in their direction. Jim and Kameswari froze and kept their heads down as far as they could.

The soldier walked through the tobacco plants and approached the hedge. Jim braced himself for sprinting or fighting or whatever might come. But the man did not notice them. He stopped, about ten yards from where they lay, and relieved himself. Then he started collecting dead branches and bamboo sticks from the hedge.

He returned to his companion holding a pile of them under his left arm. He dumped them on the ground. The other soldier lit a match. Soon they were warming themselves by the fire.

'Come, we go back. I have another plan', Kameswari announced.

'They crept back through the hole in the hedge and made their way across the mango grove to the gate.

'Stay here', Kameswari whispered. 'I'll be back soon. You're more vulnerable than me, as a foreigner.'

She climbed the gate and disappeared in the shadows of the road.

THIRTY FOUR

Half an hour later Kameswari returned to the mango grove carrying a small bundle. She climbed in over the gate.

'What's that?' Jim inquired.

'Blue saris from the Sisters', she replied. 'It's our only chance. The soldiers may let religious nuns pass through. It didn't take me long to persuade Sister Sundari to give these. She said she'd do anything to see you get out safely.'

Jim felt a lump in his throat as he held Sundari's dress. Kameswari had already begun helping him to put it on. First she turned up the hems of his trouser legs so that they would not show under the sari and rolled up the sleeves of his shirt. She fixed the petty coat over his trousers and buttoned the blouse down his chest. Then she wrapped the sari round his waist, pleating it in the front and leaving part of it to go up across his chest and over his left shoulder. The end served as a veil he could hold over his head.

When Kameswari had also finished her dressing up, they left the grove, climbing over the gate again, an acrobatic feat they could only perform, Jim discovered, by pulling up the sari over the knees. Fortunately, it was well past midnight. No one witnessed them come out to the street.

'Come with me. Keep your face covered and don't say a word!' Kameswari instructed.

They walked down the road towards the soldiers who looked up and shouted a warning.

Kameswari talked to them, an urgent note in her voice.

She's telling them we're visiting a sick person, Jim thought.

The soldiers did not know what to do. They obviously held religious Sisters in high respect. One soldier drew near to Jim and looked closer at his face.

215

'*Tellamagaru!* he exclaimed.

The other came over and also looked at Jim's face. Kameswari explained later that *tellammagaru* meant 'white Sister'. It was the expression Telugus used for European missionary nuns.

Again Kameswari pleaded, with a torrent of words.

It made an impression on the soldiers. They relented and allowed them to pass.

'Ganesh!' Kameswari muttered when they had walked far enough to be out of earshot. 'That was close. We'd almost blown it!'

Then she began to giggle.

'The Sisters who taught me would have had a fit if they'd seen me in their habit. I always was the 'enfant terrible' of their school . . . . '

The few hours they spent at the pump house were anything but comfortable. Jim would have preferred to sleep outside but Kameswari insisted he and Velamma stay in, stretched on hastily assembled mattresses of grass and straw. She and Paddy were to mount guard outside.

'Why can't we drive away further? Go back to Hyderabad?' Jim asked.

'We are waiting for Rao. He'll come in the morning', he was told.

Jim could not sleep. He was relieved when Rao eventually turned up at 3 am.

'I'm so happy both of you came through unscathed', he told Jim and Paddy. 'I was concerned about you. The last thing I wanted to happen was to lose either of you. That's also why I'm late. I had to make arrangements for your safety.'

He held a hurried consultation with Kameswari in Telugu. They were briefed about the outcome.

'I've told Kameswari to take her mother back home at the

crack of dawn when curfew will be lifted. She'll be quite safe now with soldiers throughout the village. We'll go ahead. I want to be on the road while it's still dark.'

They transferred their luggage to Rao's Landrover. Paddy took an emotional leave of Kameswari, even kissing her, to Rao's visible disgust. Jim said goodbye to Velamma.

'See you in Hyderabad!', Kameswari shouted as their car moved off in the dark.

Rao himself drove. Jim sat in the front seat next to him.

'What a bloodbath in the village', Jim commented to start a conversation.

'Indeed and it's not the end.'

'So?'

'Of course not. Madhura Reddy got a beating. He lost his wife and daughter. He is sad but he'll be clever enough to exploit the situation.'

'In what way?'

'With all those murders and no one exactly knowing who killed whom, he will get his adversaries convicted and sent to prison for life. If the police are on your side and you have the money to buy witnesses, you can eliminate almost anyone.'

'Charming!' Jim said.

'Exactly. That's why I'll stay away from the village for some time. The same applies to you. We'll have to remove all traces of your involvement.'

'How are you going to do that?'

'You're going to get a new identity.'

When morning broke they reached Yerrapandimoola, the game reserve where they had hunted on their way up to the village. They turned right into a small track that led straight into the jungle.

'This is a perfect place for breakfast', Rao announced after a twenty minutes' bumpy ride over stones and potholes. 'Moreover, I'll introduce you to some new friends who will look after you in the next phase.'

They stopped at a clearing. Jim stepped out and stretched himself, sleepy and weary. Paddy helped Rao unload a basket with food.

Suddenly two men stood before them who had come round from behind a thick bush. They carried submachine guns which they pointed straight at Jim and Paddy.

'I am Maurice Bowyer', the older one of the two said softly. 'Peter's brother. I've come to even the score.'

Jim stood paralysed. He knew this was how Peter had felt before his execution. In one final desperate thought he cried to God for mercy.

Paddy put his hand to his pocket and pulled out a revolver Kameswari must have given him. He could not complete the draw before a volley of shots sent him and Jim sprawling on the ground.

The two men stepped over and finished the job by shooting their victims at close range in the nape of the neck. Then they dragged them by their feet to a deep trench they had prepared in advance. The bodies, which were still twitching, and all Jim's and Paddy's belongings were dumped in and covered with earth.

'You will get your consignment of arms', Maurice told Rao.

Later at breakfast Maurice turned to his companion.

'I've just remembered Peter's daughter must be somewhere around in these parts. She was born to him from his Indian wife, as brown as shoe polish like herself. She wanted to marry a Fenian bastard. He gave her the shove and she became a missionary nun. She's working somewhere in the bush, like this.'

'Should we find out where she is and give her a look up?'

'Waste of time! She never belonged to us . . . . '

In Yuddhapalli many families began the sad preparations for a day of mourning and the cremation of their dead.

In the girls' hostel Sundari made an announcement.

'Children, from now on, please, call me 'Evelyn'. That was the name my father gave me. I take that name again because I know he cared for me.'

'E-ve-lene! E-ve-lene!' the children sang in chorus, dancing around her.

Sundari Evelyn picked up Shanti, the youngest of all, and kissed her on both cheeks.